HAPPINESS, LIKE WATER

Happiness, Like Water

Stories

CHINELO OKPARANTA

GRANTA

First published in Great Britain by Granta Books 2013

Granta Publications,
12 Addison Avenue, London W11 4QR

The following stories have previously been published, in
slightly different form: 'On Ohaeto Street' (*The Kenyon Review*),
'Fairness' (*Subtropics*), 'Story, Story!' (*Conjunctions*), 'Runs Girl'
('New Voices', granta.com), 'America' (*Granta*), 'Shelter' (*The
Coffin Factory*), 'Grace' (*The Southern Review*), 'Designs' (*The Iowa
Review*), 'Tumours and Butterflies' (*The Southern Review*).

A CIP catalogue record for this book
is available from the British Library

2 4 6 8 9 7 5 3 1

ISBN 978 1 84708 830 7

www.grantabooks.com

Typeset in Bembo by Patty Rennie
Printed and bound by CPI Group (UK) Ltd,
Croydon, CR0 4YY

FOR HOME

Contents

On Ohaeto Street

At the time of the robbery, Eze and Chinwe were living in the town of Elelenwo in Port Harcourt. They lived in Maewood Estates, which some of the neighbours called Ehoro's Estate, because Ehoro was the surname of the owner.

Ehoro's was a fairly large estate with about a dozen bungalows in it. The bungalows stood in clusters, separated only by gravel and grass, by the road connecting them, and by trees: orange trees, guava trees and plantain trees. There was a driveway in front of each bungalow, and each bungalow had a garage.

A cement wall rose high along the perimeter of the estate, and with it, two oversized metal gates, one at the entrance, the other at the exit. The top of the cement wall (and the tops of the adjoining gates) were lined with shards of glass – green glass, clear glass, and brown glass – the way walls and gates in Port Harcourt are still lined today.

Outside the estate, along the main road leading up to its entrance, were small shops whose owners sold Nabisco wafers and Ribena juices, tinned tomatoes and sardines in a can.

In the evenings, vendors put up makeshift stands in the spaces between the shops. There, they sold roasted corn on the cob along with native pears, and roasted plantains sprinkled with palm oil, pepper and salt.

There was a police station not too far down the road. Sometimes officers paraded back and forth in uniform.

Sometimes it was hard to tell if they were real police officers or crooks in uniform – at least, so Chinwe tells me. But it must have been true, because even as far back as then, Port Harcourt was known for its crooks.

It was her mama who encouraged them to live there, in Ehoro's estate. The same way she had encouraged Chinwe to marry Eze.

Chinwe had been living with her then, on Ohaeto Street, in the D/Line area of Port Harcourt. They lived in a small flat with yellow walls, inside and out. Chinwe was a teacher those days, home economics in St Catherine's secondary school, right there on Ohaeto Street.

The first time Eze came to them, Chinwe had just returned from work at the school. She and her mama were sitting outside on the steps to the flat, and Chinwe was telling her mama how the students wore her out, with their not being able to follow simple instructions – the way they cut the wrong sewing patterns or mixed the wrong ingredients into something as easy as the crust of a meat pie. She was saying all this when Eze walked up to them, carrying a black briefcase and a couple of magazines in his hand.

He smiled brightly and told them that his name was Eze. That he came offering the good news of God's Kingdom. Would they please invite him to tell them more?

At first Chinwe was quite annoyed by this – by the mere presence of Eze at their door, and by his request for an invitation. She frowned and shook her head, muttered to her mama to please send him away. But her mama saw some things in Eze that she liked: his crisply ironed trousers and shirt, his spotless shoes. His teeth were crooked, but in a way that her mama must have found endearing.

Her mama stood up, wiped her hands on the wrapper that was tied around her waist, stretched out her hand and shook his hand. She invited him in.

Chinwe thinks that he stayed for about an hour, but it's hard for her to know exactly how long, because after fifteen minutes of his flipping through the pages of the *Awake!* magazine, and the pages of the *Watchtower*, and the pages of his Bible (the New World Translation), she excused herself. Assignments to grade, she said, and went to her room. She fell asleep there and did not wake up until her mama came knocking at her door, asking just how long she intended to stay in her room, scolding her for being so rude to the nice young man who came to bring the good news of God's Kingdom to them.

They burst out laughing then. Because, of course, the Jehovah's Witnesses were always coming around in those days. And it was funny that they had actually invited one of them in.

'Mama, you had no business wasting his time like that!' Chinwe said.

'I know, I know,' her mama replied. And they both laughed some more.

He came back a week or so later. They were again outside on the steps. There was the scent of beans boiling on the stove. Black-eyed peas. Even outside, in the open air, he could smell it, and he told them as much. He asked if they would eat it with soaked garri or with akamu. Chinwe frowned, because she suspected he would soon invite himself for dinner. Her mama smiled and did the inviting for him.

Her papa had been a carpenter who made chairs and tables and shelves in Port Harcourt. Her mama had told her this. Chinwe had not yet been born at the time, so she had not witnessed this for herself. In any case, he was a carpenter, then for some reason or the other, he decided to become a cobbler – he needed a change of scenery perhaps. Or, maybe carpentry was wearing him out. Whatever the case, he sold all his furniture and took down the wooden CARPENTER sign on the front of his shop. He painted over the sign, and announced the place a cobbler's shop instead. He worked that way for some time – years, in fact – as a cobbler, until just before Chinwe was born.

He decided he would become a grammar-school teacher then. He had no training, but he again cleared out his shop and painted over the old sign. He made himself some chairs and desks. He found a blackboard, some chalk. He walked around town announcing the school to all the people he met. A private school, he said, for the very brightest three- to eleven-year-olds. And if they were not bright to begin with, he said, his school would make them bright.

It worked. People actually inquired. And afterwards, they actually began sending their children. Teaching was the job he stayed with until he died.

Years later, when Chinwe was old enough to care, her mama would tell Chinwe how seriously he took his teaching job, how he would come home each day with stories about the children. She told Chinwe about the way he took care to iron his trousers and his shirt, to comb his hair and pat it down, things he'd never done with either of his former jobs.

These teaching stories were mostly what her mama told Chinwe when she told the girl of her papa, and so, perhaps it was during his time working that grammar-school job that her mama loved her papa best.

He died the year Chinwe turned four, so she could barely remember him, could barely remember that grammar-school-teacher persona of his. Or rather, she remembered all of it, but only as a result of her mother's telling.

That evening with Eze standing out there, talking about beans and garri and akamu, her mama remarked on the way that Eze's shirt and trousers were always so perfectly ironed. That was the way Chinwe's papa's shirt and trousers also used to be, she said, those days he worked as a grammar-school teacher. It had a lot to do with why she was fond of Eze, she admitted. Eze laughed. Chinwe shook her head, irritated that it was such a small reason for her mama's toleration of such a large inconvenience. Little did Chinwe know that the inconvenience would grow even larger. For a while, anyway.

So, yes, her mama invited him to the beans and soaked garri dinner that night. First, he flipped through the pages of his *Watchtower*, and then through the pages of his *Awake!* In between, Chinwe observed the fancy gold watch on his wrist. She observed his crisply ironed clothes, just as her mama had observed. She noticed that they were crisply tailored, too. They appeared expensive, not quickly stitched together – certainly not the handiwork of any of the travelling tailors who paraded the roads at the time.

It was only after the magazine and Bible study was complete that Eze accepted the dinner invitation. I imagine now that he must have been enthusiastic in his acceptance. Sometimes I imagine also that he must have had an impish smile on his face.

Well, he continued to come back, the little rascal. And Chinwe actually grew accustomed to him. Sometimes she even laughed at his jokes.

He was bright – had completed an engineering programme

at the university. Civil engineering. This was why he did his evangelizing in the evenings, because during the day he worked in some division of Shell.

He had grown up a Jehovah's Witness and saw no reason to change now. There was something to be said for routines, he said. And something to be said for the fact that, just by virtue of the parents that God gave him, he had been automatically given access to this good news of God's Kingdom, which, as he said, would lead to everlasting life.

One evening, Chinwe's mother asked him what his plans were for the future. He chuckled nervously then said, 'Marriage and a family.' And then he added that he wanted the right woman, not just any woman.

'What would make her the right woman?' Chinwe's mother asked.

'Well, for one thing,' he said, 'she would have to be a Witness.'

'A witness?' she asked. 'A witness to what?'

'A Witness,' he said, stretching the word out, for emphasis. 'You know, a *Jehovah's* Witness.'

'Ah,' her mama said, very thoughtfully. And she went on to tell a story about Chinwe. She told the story in great detail. It went something like this: when Chinwe's papa was still living, and Chinwe was around three or four years old, Chinwe stumbled upon her mama's old wedding gown in the old chest where her mama stored it. She became obsessed with the gown, and with the idea of marriage, and so, starting that day, she would beg her papa to play what she called a wedding game with her. The game would usually take place in the evenings, just after dinner, when the chirping of the crickets was the loudest and could be heard clearly inside of the house. This last fact, Chinwe told me herself.

Sometimes, Chinwe tells me, she can still remember the smell of the gown: something clean and fragrant, like the scent of a freshly mopped floor. The mothballs were what caused it to smell that way. The camphor in them gave off that aroma, a mix between peppermint and cinnamon.

She'd breathe in the scent as her mama put the gown over her tiny body. I imagine it now: the way the sleeves must have extended far beyond Chinwe's fingertips, so that her mama would have to roll them up for her. The neckline was certainly more like a shoulder line on Chinwe, because Chinwe has told me that it often fell past her shoulders and all the way to the floor, and that she'd tug and tug as the ceremony was taking place, just to try to keep the dress from falling once more to the ground.

The train was the only part of the dress that was just as she liked, sprawling – more than a little like it must have been back when it trailed behind her mama. Just perfect, Chinwe would say, back then. As if the length of the train had an impact on the success of the fantasy.

It was her mama who played the part of the minister, reciting the marriage speech. *The step which you are about to take is the most important into which human beings can come . . . Do you take this girl to be your wedded wife, as long as you both shall live?* I've heard the story and imagined it enough times now to be able to describe it as if it were my own experience: her papa would nod. He'd be on his knees, so that he was only slightly taller than Chinwe. He'd be wearing a black blazer, but underneath the blazer was just the white singlet that he always wore at night, and his blue-and-white-striped pyjama pants, which came with a matching top, but whose top they hardly ever saw him wear.

'I do,' he'd say to Chinwe's mama.

Do you take this man to be your wedded husband, as long as you both shall live?

'I do,' Chinwe would say.

I now declare you husband and wife.

Her papa would lean towards her and plant a kiss on each side of her face. And then it would be time for Chinwe to go to bed.

That was the game they played, and her mama told Eze as much.

Then one evening, just before they were to play the game, Jehovah's Witnesses came knocking on their door, and Chinwe's papa was inviting them in, but she, Chinwe's mother, scolded him, in front of them, for even thinking to invite them in. Did he know that they were a cult? she asked.

He politely withdrew his invitation and sent them away. It was the first time that Jehovah's Witnesses had ever come to their door, and that was the treatment they received, thanks to her. So, she reasoned, perhaps this was that old story coming full circle. Perhaps this was God allowing her to make amends for that former discourtesy. And given that the discourtesy took place during one of the wedding-game nights, maybe all of that was a sign, a harbinger of things to come.

She smiled widely as she said all this, and Eze smiled with her.

Chinwe's mother herself never did become a Witness. Instead she encouraged Chinwe to become one, so that Chinwe would indeed marry the nice young man who was obviously well-to-do, and who would obviously provide for her, who only wanted for himself a Witness wife. Was it too much to ask? No, said Chinwe's mother, responding to her own question, earnestly shaking her head.

They did in fact marry, a year and a half after he first offered Chinwe and her mother the good news of God's Kingdom. Chinwe was very dutiful about the wedding. On the surface her dutifulness must have looked like excitement. Perhaps it was.

It was a large celebration, held at the Kingdom Hall on Rumuola Road. His parents and family members attended, along with his Jehovah's Witness friends, whom he also referred to as family – as 'brothers' and 'sisters'.

Theirs was only a white wedding; no traditional one. Even the white wedding was relatively brief, and very sedate, a fact for which Chinwe might or might not have been grateful. It's hard to know.

It was after their wedding that Chinwe's mama encouraged them to live in Ehoro's Estate. By this time, Chinwe had given up her teaching job 'to take on more fully the role of a wife', as her mama liked to explain it. Eze was the one who insisted on this to begin with (after all, they planned on having children soon and who would take care of the children if Chinwe kept up that job of hers?). Her mama had, of course, agreed.

In any case, her mama encouraged them to live in Ehoro's Estate for two reasons. First, Elelenwo was not too far from D/Line. That is, it was far enough for Chinwe and Eze to feel separate, to feel independent from her, but it was close enough that she could hop on a bus and come visit whenever she wanted. (This ease of access would be a good thing when they decided to have a child, she said.) Secondly, she reasoned that Ehoro's Estate was a swanky neighbourhood, just up Eze's alley; and if they lived there, she could vicariously experience the good life through them.

It was true about the estate's swankiness. Those days, the driveways and garages in Ehoro's were filled with Volvos and

Jeeps and BMWs. The yards were well manicured, and the families took turns hosting elegant dinner parties where people dressed in their finest traditional or European/American attire.

After they moved in, Eze got himself a Land Rover. But that must not have been enough, because he soon got himself a 505 SRS, which rivalled the BMW in many ways, or at least Eze said it did. Chinwe continued to drive her little yellow Volkswagen Beetle, which was just fine by her.

After the car came (the 505 SRS), Eze joined the residents in hosting those dinner parties. His parties were attended mostly by neighbourhood people, but sometimes his work friends also came. Every once in a while, people from the Kingdom Hall attended too. In the months right after the 505 SRS came, Eze hosted those parties with greater frequency than ever, inviting as many people as he possibly could, as if he were on a mission to show off the car to them all in the shortest amount of time possible.

Chinwe and the housegirls would make trays of spicy suya – skewered beef, and chicken, and fish, all flavoured with groundnuts – and they would fry up large pans of sweet chin chin, and bake batches of meat pies and sausage rolls. Eze would set out crates of Guinness and soft drinks.

This was the way it worked: first, the people would enter the house. If Chinwe happened to be standing at the entrance, they'd walk right past her, straight to where Eze stood, and they'd tell Eze what a lovely home he had. At the onset, it certainly pleased Chinwe, the way they oohhed and aahhed – it was after all her home as well. It pleased her that they admired the entertainment centre, referring to the things in it as 'state of the art electronics'. They'd stand, so many of them that there was barely enough space to move around. They'd eat the food that Chinwe and the housegirls had prepared. Then

Chinwe would watch as Eze took out his keys, as he walked the men especially out to the front yard, as he opened up the 505 and showed them the interior. Sometimes, when Chinwe's mama came, she joined the men in oohhing and aahhing over the house, over the car. As if she'd not seen it all before. Those sorts of things pleased her very much.

Well, needless to say, Ehoro's Estate became a target for robbers. Months before the robbers came, the residents of Ehoro's had held a meeting, suspecting that it was only a matter of time before they, too, were hit. There had been rumours as to the identities of the band of thieves, and so, during that meeting, the residents proposed that a collection be started. The plan was to make a peace offering to the robbers, to thwart their attempts on the estate. The residents all agreed that this was a more effective solution – better than, say, reporting the thieves to the police, which some said would only serve to ignite their anger. Also, with so many fake police officers running all over the place, who was to say that they wouldn't be filing the report with the very robbers whom they were trying to apprehend? So the money offering was decided upon. The residents went about putting in their contributions. Everyone contributed. Everyone, except Eze.

Not that he was stingy, he said, but it went against his morals and values. A collection like that was a way of condoning bad behaviour, and so they should count him out. Chinwe believed that Eze should have paid his share. Or else he should have moved them out to a less fancy neighbourhood and should have driven less fancy cars, not the 505 SRS or the Land Rover. Something less flashy, like Chinwe's Beetle, or like a 504 or one of the old Fords.

But he did none of that.

★

By then, Chinwe had been baptized a Jehovah's Witness, but it was a thing she had done out of duty to Eze. He had insisted on it, had even grown cross with her when she appeared to suggest otherwise. After all, he said, it had been a condition of the marriage from the beginning. And so Chinwe conceded. Of course, her concession pleased her mama.

Chinwe attended the meetings with Eze: once a week, on Tuesdays, their congregation broke into small groups and met for Bible study at the houses of different elders. But for the remaining Bible study days (Thursdays, Saturdays and Sundays), they met at the Kingdom Hall.

The meetings began with a song, which they all sang, accompanied by the music that came from the cassette player at the back of the room. Then they'd sit and listen to the elder on stage who read from the New World Translation. This lecture took about an hour and sometimes Chinwe would stare at the walls and trace the cracks that ran along them, over and over again. It was a game she played with herself, to keep from falling asleep. Because whenever she fell asleep, Eze grew angry at her. He'd nudge her awake and then shake his head re-proachfully at her right there in the Kingdom Hall. Sometimes, when they got home, he made jokes (he'd later call them jokes, anyway) about flogging her with a belt for having fallen asleep. Because she needed to learn to be more respectful to God, he said. And the first step in showing respect was to stay awake during discussions on God.

The evening the robbers came, Chinwe and Eze had attended the Kingdom Hall. She'd not fallen asleep, so Eze had not scolded her afterwards about that. But the story goes that, when they returned home, she went in to work in the kitchen with the housegirls, to prepare dinner. Somehow, for one

reason or another, the meal had turned out too spicy. In fact
there was the hot scent of crushed peppers in the air
throughout the bungalow. And, when she and Eze sat down to
eat, their tongues seethed from the heat of the peppers. That
gave Eze all the reason he needed to be cross with her.

That night – the night of the robbery – Chinwe fell asleep
in a sad state, still smarting from Eze's scolding. She fell asleep
to the sound of the floor fan, which stood at the corner of
the room, humming softly with each oscillation, like a lullaby.
Usually, she opened their bedroom windows halfway at night,
and as she fell asleep, she listened to the sounds of the guava and
plantain trees just outside, their leaves rustling in the breeze.
But that night the air was still. And with the scent of crushed
peppers strong in the air, travelling down their nostrils and into
their throats, causing them all to cough drily, something had to
be done. It followed that Chinwe turned on the fan and
opened the windows all the way. Also, she left the door to their
room open, the door that led to the corridor.

She awoke to the sound of shattering glass and to the sight
of two men entering the room. The room was dark, but owing
to the moonlight which crept in through the open windows,
she could see that the men were masked. There was a metal
safe that Eze kept in the bottom shelf of the bedside table. One
of the men went straight to the safe, picked it up, pointed the
gun at Eze, ordered him to open up the safe. Of course, Eze
refused.

The man held the gun even closer to Eze's head. There was
a clicking sound. That was when Chinwe screamed, begging
the man to stop. The second man, who had until then been
lingering at the doorway, made his way to her side then. She
could not see the look on his face owing to the mask that he
wore, but it must have been sympathetic, because he tapped

her on the shoulder and told her not to worry, that everything would be fine if she would only open the safe for him.

So she grabbed the safe from Eze, dialled the combination and opened it up herself. She spilled its contents onto the white bedding: tangled-up necklaces of gold, rings whose jewels shone in the dark. And then, of course, there were the wads and wads of naira bills, which the men stuck into the bags that hung from their shoulders.

'Good work,' the second man said, patting her on the shoulder when he was done bagging the items. But still, his gun found its way behind her head.

So, that night, the men hold their guns behind Chinwe's and Eze's heads, and lead them out into the corridor. Chinwe watches as Eze struggles with his man, refusing to move so that the man has to shove him forward. She knows that the house-girls are in the quarters at the back of the house. She wills them to appear, to somehow appear and scare the robbers away. She wills them to hear, but it doesn't seem that they hear a thing.

Chinwe and Eze stand quietly in the corridor for a while, Chinwe listening to the sound of the oscillating fan in their room. Even though it is a distance away, its sound is loud, because, of course, everything is quiet now. (This is also the first time the two robbers appear to communicate with each other, but even that is a silent sort of communication, one which they do solely with their eyes.)

After the silence, the man holding the gun to Eze's head says: 'That car outside, the white one, we'll be needing the keys.'

Eze has a look of horror in his face, as if he's just seen death, which is funny, because until then, he's been acting bold and courageous, resisting and all.

'The keys,' the man repeats. 'And actually, we'll also be needing you to come out and start it for us.'

One can only imagine the emotions Eze must have been feeling inside, because that car was his prized possession. (Every once in a while, before the robbery, that is, he'd taken to reminding Chinwe that it was the only one of its kind in the whole of Rivers State, that there were only two of them in the whole of Nigeria, the other owner being a 'big' man, a governor of one of the other states.)

In any case, the robber has to drag Eze again in order to get him to move, smacking Eze's head every so often with the gun. 'Start the car, and no wahala for you; don't start the car, and we'll shoot,' the man says as he drags Eze.

Chinwe and Eze manage to make eye contact somewhere in the middle of all the dragging and head smacking. Chinwe looks at Eze with pleading eyes. *Just give them the car. Give them the car and spare our lives.* But the more she looks at him, the more defeat she feels, because she knows that she's no match for the car.

So she just stands there, watching the man drag Eze outside. She remains inside with the second robber still pointing his gun at her head. But even if she is inside, she knows what things are like outside: the ground paved with gravel and grass, and the bush near where the 505 is parked – green, saturated with the red of the hibiscus flowers. She and Eze stood in front of that bush for a picture on the day that Eze brought home the 505 SRS.

It was her mama who took the picture. Here and there lizards were crawling over the gravel stones. As she stands there, with the robber holding a gun to her head, she remembers her mama holding the camera, taking a picture of her and Eze, and of the car. And somehow, she thinks of the wedding game she used to play with her papa. Suddenly, she imagines that if the camera could have spoken the day her mama took the picture, it would have said something like this: *The step which you are about to take is the most important into which you will come . . . Do you take this car to be your wedded wife, as long as you both shall live?* And Eze would nod ecstatically at the camera, and he would fervently say, 'I do.'

And that answer would be correct.

In any case, the way she tells the story, some more time passes, quiet time, and Chinwe allows herself to get lost in her thoughts. She moves on from the memory of the wedding game, and she remembers that the police station is not too far down the street. She starts to think that maybe one of the real police officers will somehow see or hear something. She also thinks of Ehoro, the estate's owner. She remembers that he had begun carrying a gun the moment the threat of the robbers became real, around the time they held that 'anti-robbery collection' meeting. She becomes hopeful that someone, either a real police officer, or Ehoro himself, will come to the rescue.

She hears the gunshot then. She shrieks, as if the bullet had been fired at her, as if it were piercing her own body.

The story goes that after the robber leads Eze to the 505 SRS (somehow the man gets Eze to produce the key), the man opens the car door, asks Eze to enter and to start the car. Eze gets in, puts the key into the ignition, but the car refuses to start. The man asks him to try again. Eze turns the key in the ignition, the engine makes a squeaking sound, but it still does not start. Meanwhile, Eze holds his hands up in the air, at the sides of his face, shakes his head, continues to shake it, as if he does not know why the car won't start.

The man pulls Eze out of the car, drags him to the Land Rover, which is on the other side of the front yard. He believes that Eze is purposefully doing something to prevent the car from starting (and he is right). In any case, when he's dragged Eze to the Land Rover, he asks Eze to raise his hands over his head, all the way up, as if Eze himself is the criminal, as if he is under arrest.

The man steps back so that there is some distance between him and Eze. Then he aims the gun at Eze. Maybe he is just about to fire when he hears the gunshot. Maybe he had no intention of firing at all – just a little something to scare Eze into starting the 505. Whatever the case, Eze's robber hears the gunshot too, and suddenly he is on the tips of his toes, running away with his gun, across the front yard, even jumping over the glass-lined gate of the estate to escape.

At least, this is how Eze told the story of what happened outside.

Inside, after they hear the shot, the robber who is holding the gun to Chinwe's head lowers his gun. He appears confused, puzzled, then he turns to the door that leads to the garage and out to the driveway, and he too runs off.

There is some screaming outside, and the sound of racing feet, but Chinwe stays inside and just waits, too stunned even to know what she is waiting for.

Not very long after, Mr Ehoro enters the corridor with Eze by his side. There is sweat dripping from Ehoro's forehead, and he wipes it with the back of his hand. There is sweat also dripping from Eze's forehead, but Chinwe pays that no mind. Instead, she looks for the blood on Eze's chest. But there is none.

Eze starts to tell the story of what happened outside then, how he refused to start the car by not pressing one of the buttons he should have pressed first before inserting the key into the ignition. He laughs at his cleverness. He winks at Chinwe, a self-congratulatory wink, as if to say, 'Aren't I something?' It is now Friday, and Eze laments that it is not Thursday all over again, or Saturday, or Sunday, so that he can tell the story at once to the entire congregation at the Kingdom Hall. For now, his imagination will have to do, and so he imagines breaking the news, and he anticipates what their reaction will be – gratitude to God for the miracle.

Chinwe listens to him for some time. Ehoro stands by Eze's side, listening too. Sometimes he laughs at the things Eze says.

'I'm leaving,' Chinwe says, numbly. It comes out as a whisper, and Eze continues to speak, because he doesn't hear her.

She turns around and heads for their bedroom. The fan is still oscillating, and the metal safe lies open on their bed, empty. She moves it aside gently. She goes to her wardrobe, opens it, takes out a large suitcase from its bottom shelf. She removes a few of her clothes from their hangers, folds them one by one and puts them into the suitcase. She is still folding the items when she hears the sound of Eze's footsteps approaching. She sits on the bed, by the open suitcase, and waits for him to walk into the room. As she waits, she imagines that he is already inside the room, that he has made his way to her in the still dark room. She imagines that he wrinkles his forehead, like a question, and reaches out with his arms to stop her from what she is doing.

She imagines him telling her that she will break her mother's heart by leaving him. Telling her that even her mother would want to know the meaning of all this. (Of course, he would be right.)

She imagines that he runs off to find his New World Translation, and that he returns with it, and he reads from it to her, about marriage, about God's disapprobation of divorce.

She even imagines him asking her how she expects to

survive without a job, without any income. 'A grown woman like you living off your mama?' she imagines him saying. When he asks it, she does not bother to respond. Instead, she thinks of herself back at her teaching job, and she thinks how grateful she will be to be back.

In her imagination, Eze continues to chide, but she continues to pack her bag. When it is all packed, she lifts it from the bed and only pauses to say goodbye.

She sits there and imagines all this, and she waits. But it is a long while before he enters the room, and a long time before she musters the courage to zip up the suitcase and leave.

It is an even longer time before we meet each other by chance on Ohaeto Street; and it is a bit more time before Chinwe decides – without her mother's influence – that she will try her hand at marriage again, this time by becoming *my* wife.

Wahala!

The healing was a thing that Ezinne's mother, Nneka, told Chibuzo about weeks ago, nearly a month now. Afterwards, on the same night of the telling, he dreamed of it.

In his dream, he watched the entire process as if watching it on a television screen. But it was not on a television screen that he watched it, rather on an old, brittle bar of Ivory soap.

It was not easy watching the healing on the bar of soap: the images were small, and had missing portions in them – those places where fissures had formed on the soap, a result of desiccation. The fissures made it hard for him to see, but even without them, the viewing would have been difficult still, because the images were themselves like soap when wet: slippery, with bubbles all around, dissolving and hard to grasp.

In the dream, his trouble viewing the images was what caused Chibuzo to pay a visit to the native doctor. He went to her in order to see if she could show them to him on something better than the bar of soap. He asked to see it on a kom kom of evaporated milk, after its paper label had been peeled off, or even just on the surface of a drinking gourd; and she, the dibia, did in fact show it to him more clearly: as he requested, on the can of evaporated milk.

Now he stood by the kitchen door, bidding the visitors goodbye. Ezinne's mother, Nneka, stood by his side.

The kitchen smelled of tomato stew, the thin kind, with peppers and spices mixed in, but thin because it had been made with more water than usual, so that it would be enough to feed the mass of invited guests. (The guests had eaten the stew with rice, and afterwards they had chased the meal down with jugs of palm wine.)

The purpose of the dinner was to ensure that Chibuzo's wife, Ezinne, had the well-wishes, and sympathy, and even the gratitude of the neighbours. Because everyone knew what happened to Mbachu's wife: first, going so many years without getting with child, and then finally getting with child only to lose it.

It had been all over town, this case of Mbachu's wife. Some said that her childlessness was due to the malice of jealous neighbours (Mbachu's wife was after all very beautiful). Or perhaps her childlessness was simply a result of a general indifference on the part of the townspeople. Surely, the rumours said, apathy had a way of creating negative energy, and this negative energy had the ability to reinforce itself in the barrenness of one's womb.

Mbachu's relatives eventually began prodding him to leave his wife and take another, one who could give him children, sons especially, to carry on the family name. Some time around then, his wife became with child. It was serendipitous, and owing to it, the rumours died down.

But then, just as unexpectedly, it was announced that she had lost the child. This loss reignited the rumours, which then persisted well beyond the day that Mbachu cast her off, beyond the day that Mbachu took another wife, even beyond the day, years later, that this new wife bore him a son.

The idea of malice and negative energy made sense to Chibuzo. And anyway, who was he to go against this collective explanation? It was after all agreed upon by so many. Who was he to say that malice and apathy weren't indeed potential causes of barrenness?

And so, the dinner: so that Chibuzo could avert any malice or negativity that was being directed at Ezinne. So that he could divert from her a fate similar to that of Mbachu's wife.

They had been sitting in the parlour when Nneka told Chibuzo of the healing. It was night time, and NEPA had taken light, so it was dark all around, except for the small flame of the candle that sat on a denuded kom kom.

Nneka told him the story very simply: that she herself had gone to a dibia, a long time ago. She'd gone for the same reasons that she was recommending the dibia for Ezinne: because a long time ago, she too had been unable to conceive. It was only thanks to the dibia that she was finally able to get with child – finally able to beget Ezinne, which was lucky, because, had she not, there was a good chance that Ezinne's father – God rest his soul – would have cast her away and taken another wife. She would not have blamed him, she said. After all, what kind of man was content to keep an mgbaliga, an empty barrel, as a wife?

Ezinne was in the bedroom when Nneka made the revelation. The room was down the corridor, past the kitchen.

Ezinne was also in the bedroom now, weeks later. The dinner had worn her out, physically – because she was after all the one who made the preparations for it (with just a little help from Nneka and from the housegirls). It had been mentally exhausting too, because all the while her mind had been heavy with the knowledge that she was the subject of the dinner, that some imperfection in her was the reason for all that wahala, all that trouble. And what if the imperfection was not really even in her? What if it was in *him*? It was a thought that she could not dare voice. It was generally understood that such things were the fault of the woman.

Earlier this morning, just at the break of dawn, they had all three of them driven to the dibia's. (Chibuzo had gone along on the visit. It was in his best interest to do so, he said. Besides, it was a Saturday. He could afford to go along, not having the constraint of work.)

The dibia's place was in the outskirts of Port Harcourt, one of the villages at nearly an hour's drive from Rumuola. The road leading directly into the village was made of earth, not paved with tar like all the roads that came before. Green and yellow grass stood on either side of it, the blades rising high, as tall as small children. And then there were the goats, fading in and out of the grass, and the cows, and the chickens, and also the dogs.

Emmanuel, Nneka's chauffeur, was the one who drove them there. Every once in a while, he turned a corner and exclaimed, 'Sorry o! Ndo!' because, in those parts where the green grass grew high, and the cornstalks stood even taller than the grass, it was hard for him to see the cows. And so, coming out of several turns, he'd very nearly hit a cow, and he'd slam force-fully on the brakes, and there'd be that sudden jerk of the SUV, followed by his apology. It was indeed a bumpy ride. But even-tually they arrived.

The dibia practised in one corner of her veranda. In another corner she sold snacks – sweets, Nabisco wafers, chewing gum, groundnuts, as well as the oils and roots she used in her healing.

The veranda was made of grey cement. Its roof was an extension of the main house's roof: it was made of thatch, and of patches of zinc. A railing ran around the front of the veranda, like a half-wall. In the corner where there were no items to be sold sat a stool, and to the side of the stool – on the veranda's railing – a jerrycan of water, a clear drinking glass and a straw, which rose like a buoy from inside the glass.

It was hot on the veranda, but it was a dry sort of heat, no mugginess to it. In the horizon, the sky was a soft blue. Despite her hopelessness, Ezinne noticed this. Or perhaps it was owing to her hopelessness that she noticed. It was a soft blue sky, but there were streaks of white in it, large streaks, a little like over-sized feathers.

The dibia was a small woman with grey hair and teeth that must have, long ago, resulted in a beautiful smile. But now her teeth were cracked and yellowed, and her lips were tightened and wrinkled, remnants of old beauty. She wore thin gold bangles on her wrist. They jingled and chimed as she moved her arm, as she waved Ezinne over to take a seat on the stool.

Ezinne told the dibia of the pain. She said that it came in her lower belly each time Chibuzo inserted himself into her. It hadn't always been there, she explained. It had come on suddenly, one of the nights that she lay with Chibuzo, some months after they were wed. Perhaps it was a thing that happened because she had by then already begun to grow afraid of not being able to bear Chibuzo a child. In any case, each time afterwards that he made to enter her, she stiffened, and there was the pain. Or rather, she said, it was hard to tell which one came first – the stiffening or the pain.

The dibia listened. She nodded sparingly as Ezinne explained, and then she responded that, whatever the issue, whether it was pain or just fear, she was sure she could cause it to disappear.

'Amen!' Nneka exclaimed from where she sat at the rear of the veranda.

Chibuzo, seated there by Nneka's side, did not say a word.

Ezinne exhaled.

On the railing, near where the jerrycan and glass and straw sat, were also two glass bottles of oils, with brown roots or some plant-like substances in them. The dibia took the smaller of the two bottles, twisted off the cap, poured a bit of the oil into her hand. With her fingers, she dabbed the oil on Ezinne – on her forehead, on the sides of her face, on the back of her neck, on her chest (the triangle of skin which the deep V-neck of her blouse made visible). The air smelled of manure, of cow dung, and Ezinne breathed it all in and allowed herself to be dabbed. She leaned her back into the railing of the veranda – the part of it where there were no items in the way.

The dibia moved on from the oil. She raised the glass and straw, rinsed them using the water in the jerrycan. She rinsed holding them over the veranda's railing, so that the water poured outside the veranda, onto the grass and gravel there. Afterwards, she shook out the glass and straw as if to dry them. She blew through the straw, as if to get rid of any latent sediment. Then she filled the glass nearly to its brim with the water from the jerrycan. She stuck the straw into the water in the glass. She was ready then to proceed with the healing.

Chibuzo sat by Nneka and watched. So far, it was just as Nneka had explained it would be. And it was just as Chibuzo had dreamt it would be.

The dibia brought the glass, the straw still in it, to the side of Ezinne's face. She blew into the straw so that bubbles formed in the water. She brought the glass to the other side of Ezinne's face. She blew into the straw again, so that more bubbles formed. The water turned a little cloudy. Just as in the dream.

She brought the glass to Ezinne's chest and continued to blow into the straw. She lowered the glass slowly downwards, lingering in the area of Ezinne's belly, and then lower. She blew and blew.

Ezinne watched the dibia. She took in the wrinkles on the woman's face – the way the age spots blemished her skin like dark stars on the surface of a light-coloured sky. She took in the seriousness of the dibia's face, and the deep purple of the blouse the dibia wore, deep purple like a bruise, Ezinne thought.

Every once in a while, Ezinne closed her eyes and simply listened to the cracking of the bubbles, and to the jingling of the dibia's bangles as they bumped one against another and around the dibia's wrist.

The dibia continued to blow. The water in the glass became cloudier – a foamy sort of cloudiness, a little like palm wine. Then suddenly the liquid was becoming yellowish, and then there was sediment visible in it – small brownish particles, which floated and multiplied inside the glass.

The dibia stopped. She raised the glass, peered at it, used the straw to prod the particles in the liquid. She shook her head in dismay. She said, 'Not good. Not good at all.'

'What?' Ezinne asked, alarmed. Her mother had by now gotten up from where she sat waiting in the rear of the room. Chibuzo stood too. They approached Ezinne and the dibia. *What is the matter?* their faces seemed to ask.

The dibia continued to shake her head, continued to prod the particles in the glass. Finally, she stuck her hand into the liquid and pulled out one of the small brownish particles in it. She inspected the particle with her fingers, turned it this way and that, brought it closer to her eyes. Some sand had come out with the particle. She wiped off the sand, and then she said, 'These are the impurities in you. Fish scale. Sand.' She was still inspecting the particle as she spoke. She finished, 'You've been cursed by the enchanted.'

'Cursed by the enchanted?' Chibuzo asked. This part was not as he had dreamt.

Nneka began to whimper.

Ezinne sat quietly, stunned.

'Cursed by the enchanted?' Chibuzo asked again.

The dibia nodded. 'The spirits,' she said. 'They curse us sometimes for no reason at all. Or sometimes they curse us because something or someone has inadvertently angered them. Or sometimes simply because they are in a bad mood.' She paused. 'Don't worry. I will clean you of their curses. I will make you well again.' With that, she lowered her hand, flicked off the particle. She turned to the railing and poured out the water from the glass. She rinsed out the glass, rinsed out the straw. She leaned over Ezinne once more, having poured new water from the jerrycan into the glass. She began again to blow.

That second round, the water grew even cloudier than the first, and the particles were larger, and had multiplied. The dibia inspected them again and announced that in addition to the sand and fish scale, there were now small bits of tree bark and red plastic in the water.

Nneka and Chibuzo stood more alarmed than before. Ezinne sat startled; tears rolled down her cheeks. No-one spoke. The dibia began the third round.

In the rounds that followed, the water grew decreasingly cloudy. By the sixth round, even with all her blowing, the water remained clean and clear.

The dibia finished by dabbing some more healing oil on Ezinne's forehead, and face, and neck. She collected her payment. For three hundred additional naira, she gave Ezinne an unopened bottle of oil, which, she said, if used daily, would ward off any further curses of the enchanted.

Ezinne stood up. Chibuzo wrapped his arm around her. She leaned, a bit hesitantly, into him. They walked that way to the car. Nneka trailed behind, a weak but hopeful smile on her face.

It was noon by the time they got back home. The sun was

high in the sky and painted the tips of the trees and the roof-tops a bright yellow. Chibuzo again wrapped his arm around Ezinne's waist and escorted her into the house.

They were eating lunch – garri and soup, which the house-girls had prepared – when Nneka announced that they should host the dinner. Tonight, she said, because why waste any time? Her eyes were bright with excitement, the eyes of a woman with a plan.

At first Chibuzo was quite in disagreement, because he could see how upset the healing had made Ezinne. But then he reasoned that the dinner – the company and socialization that came with it – would help to take Ezinne's mind off all that had transpired on the dibia's veranda. And, by the end of the night, if the dinner was a success, Ezinne would be feeling less upset and perhaps even eager to get to work as far as the conception of the child was concerned. What with all the safety measures having been taken – the healing and then the precautionary dinner – he could see no reason why she wouldn't be eager. He said all this as they sat at the table. Nneka nodded fervently. Ezinne looked down despairingly into her bowl of soup.

And so it was set. Chibuzo sent the two housegirls to invite all the residents of their Rumuola neighbourhood. As it was a Saturday, chances were that many of the residents would be home, lounging around. Evening was still six or seven hours away, more than enough time to do all the inviting, and just enough time to prepare the meal.

As far as the preparations went, he himself set out to the market down the road from their house. There he purchased several hens to be used for the meal. He delivered the hens to Ezinne and Nneka in the kitchen. He had done his duty. Ezinne and Nneka, along with the housegirls, would do the rest.

Before the meal, Chibuzo had come into the kitchen to

take a look at the food. Rice filled two large pots almost to the brim. Meat filled the other two pots, the feet of the hens sticking out of the red stew like leafless branches from the ground. Chibuzo inhaled deeply, smiled, patted Ezinne on the back. This was his way of letting her know how pleased he was with the food.

They dressed quickly, Chibuzo in his gold-trimmed agbada, Nneka in her lace blouse and aso oke wrappers. Ezinne wore a straight-cut brocade gown, out of which Nneka insisted she change, because the dress was too plain, she said. But the guests arrived promptly, and Ezinne was spared the change.

The guests strolled into the house dressed more in the fashion of Chibuzo and Nneka – in fancy attire. The housegirls let them in, but it was Ezinne who showed them the way to the table, where Chibuzo and Nneka were seated and eager to regale.

It was a struggle for Ezinne to keep the smile on her face. She wanted nothing more than to escape, to sneak into the bedroom and drift into sleep.

But it was her duty to serve the meal, and so she did, recruiting the help of the housegirls only where the distribution of the plates was concerned.

Now Chibuzo, standing by the door, bids goodbye to the guests. As they file out, he thinks how successful the dinner was. The lids of the pots lie idle on the countertop, and the pots themselves are on the stove, empty, or nearly so – all that remains in them are a few grains of rice and what might amount to a few teaspoons of stew. He thinks of the dinner's success, but mostly he is impatient for the guests to leave.

Nneka stands at her son-in-law's side, leaning on the door, ushering the guests out with a smile. It is not the kind of smile that would be expected of her – it is, rather, the kind that would be expected of Ezinne: a forced smile. The reason for this change in Nneka is that she is no longer in the mood to regale. She is now impatient for the guests to leave, for the same reason that Chibuzo is impatient too: because Ezinne has disappeared, and they will have to hurry the guests off if Chibuzo is to stand a chance of making it to Ezinne in time.

When the last guest is gone, Chibuzo leans on the door for a moment, exhales loudly. Nneka pats him swiftly on the shoulder, and just as swiftly, he is off.

In the room, it is dark, but there is a little light coming from the window, so that Chibuzo can just make out the outline of Ezinne's body on the bed.

'Hey,' he says, light-heartedly, as he enters. He swings the door behind him to shut it, but the door does not exactly close. There is a small gap where it does not quite meet the frame. He does not notice this.

He takes a seat on her side of the bed, the side closest to the door. Ezinne moves a little to make room for him. She is lying on her stomach, her arms folded beneath her face. She turns to look at him.

'Long day,' he says, like a sigh, moving his hand up and down her back.

'Yes, very long day,' she says. 'I'm tired.'

He laughs a little, awkwardly. She can hear the unease in his laughter.

He gets into bed with her, fully clothed, presses his body hard against hers. His hands make their way to her hips. 'Yes,' he says. 'Makes sense that you'd be tired.' He pauses. 'But you can't be too tired yet,' he says. 'There's one more thing to do.' He laughs again, softly.

She turns her head away from him, struggles free from him a little. 'Not now,' she says. 'Not tonight.' She says it boldly, though from the tension in his body she speculates that it is a losing battle.

And of course she is right.

'Yes, tonight,' he says. His voice is gravelly and firm.

She closes her eyes, but she can still see him in her mind's eye. She sees his square jaw. It is taut, stiff. She sees his mouth rounded with determination. She sees his arms underneath the shirt that he is wearing. They are slender, almost scrawny, but she knows that there is strength in them – more strength than their size suggests. She knows this strength for herself, and so she moves a little farther from him. 'Please, Chibuzo,' she says. 'Not tonight.'

'But we need to try,' he says. 'You know, I'm a patient man, but my patience is running out. How do you think this is making me look? A man like me, of my status, and yet with no child to show for it.' He pauses. Softer, he says, almost pleading, 'We need a child, not even a son. A girl is fine. We need a child, or this marriage is null.'

With that, he nudges her to turn around. First he holds her face in his hands and places kisses on her forehead, on her cheeks, on the tip of her nose, on her lips. Then his hands make their way to her thighs. He lifts the skirt of her nightgown gently. He strokes her, whispers to her to relax, and she does.

Soon, she hears the unzipping of his trousers. He climbs on top of her. She tenses up, and somehow he feels it. 'It's okay,' he says. 'It's okay.' He strokes her face with one hand.

She relaxes again. 'Okay,' she says.

There are tears in her eyes by now, but she blinks them away. She allows him to continue. 'Okay,' she says again, but as he enters her, there is the pain, sharp and as wilful as ever before.

She moans, but he enters anyway. He thrusts himself into and out of her, and she continues to moan, louder and louder. 'Please!' she finally screams, but he doesn't seem to hear. She tries again. 'Chibuzo, please stop!'

He thrusts. He thinks of the dibia, her cleansing of Ezinne. He thinks of the dinner, the way the guests ate gratefully, the well-wishes they gave as they left. He feels elated, optimistic. It is dark in the room, but for him there is light.

'Please,' she says again.

He hears her moaning, her cries, but he hears it softer than it has been in the past – softer in the midst of all that radiance.

Please.

He takes in all the pleading, but what he hears are gentle sounds of pleasure, not at all sounds of pain. He does not hear the 'stop' that comes after the 'please'. He thrusts, with the desire to gratify, and all the while he is envisioning the future: he sees himself holding his son or his daughter, a baby. He is holding the baby when its umbilical cord stump falls off. He is holding the baby all the days when the baby teethes. And when the child is old enough, he carries the child on his shoulders. He watches as the child climbs the orange and guava trees outside in their backyard, as the child plucks the hibiscus flowers from the bushes in the compound, as the child picks pebbles to play with its catapult. He sees the day the child begins to go to school – the uniform the child wears, green and white, like the colour of the flag. The child is happy. And Chibuzo, imagining the child, is happy too.

Ezinne continues to moan from the pain, moans so loudly that even Nneka hears. By this time, Nneka has distributed the clean-up work amongst the housegirls, and has left them to it. She heads towards Chibuzo and Ezinne's room, crouches down by the slightly open door and listens in on them. The air in the corridor where she is crouched smells of Ezinne's stew. Nneka's clothes, too, carry the scent of the stew. For a moment Nneka thinks that she should go and change out of her clothes, that she should go prepare herself for bed; after all, she is tired, too.

But she remains by the door, hopeful and anxious at once. She narrows her eyes in order to see better through the gap. She peers, but Chibuzo and Ezinne are hard to grasp – there are missing portions in their images, those places where darkness has asserted itself.

Still, Nneka peers. She widens her eyes. She blinks as if to blink some clarity into the scene. Finally, she surrenders, resigns herself to only listening.

Ezinne's moaning continues. It grows louder. Nneka takes in the moaning, takes in the increasing loudness of it. She nods approvingly, happiness overwhelming. She smiles widely, because, unsurprisingly, she hears it the same way that Chibuzo does: sounds of pleasure, rather than sounds of pain.

Fairness

We gather outside the classroom in the break between morning and afternoon lectures. We stand on the concrete steps, chewing groundnuts and meat pies, all of us with the same dark skin, matching, like the uniforms we wear. All of us, excepting Onyechi of course, because her skin has now turned colour, and we are eager to know how. It is the reason she stands with us, though she no longer belongs. She is now one of the others, one of the girls with fair skin.

Clara looks at Onyechi, her eyes narrow, a suspicious look. Boma chuckles in disbelief. She claps her hands, her eyes widen. She exclaims, 'chi m o! My God! How fast the miracle!' Onyechi shakes her head, tells us that it was no miracle at all. It is then that she tells us of the bleach. Boma chuckles again. I think of Eno, of returning home and telling her what Onyechi has said. I listen and nod, trying to catch every bit of the formula. Clara says, 'I don't believe it.' Onyechi kisses the palm of her right hand and raises it high towards the sky, a swear to God, because she insists that she is not telling a lie. Our skin is the colour not of ripe pawpaw peels, but of its seeds. We are thirsty for fairness. But even with her swearing, we are unconvinced, a little too disbelieving of what Onyechi has said.

Hours later, I sit on a stool outside, in the backyard of our house. I sit under the mango tree, across from the hibiscus bush. Ekaite is at the far end of the backyard where the clotheslines hang. She collects Papa's shirts from the line, a row of them, which wave in the breeze like misshapen flags. Even in the near darkness, I can see the yellowness of Ekaite's skin. A natural yellow, not like Onyechi's or some of the other girls'. Not like Mama's.

Eno sits with me, and at first we trace the lizards with our eyes. We watch as they race up and down the gate. We watch as they scurry over the gravel, over the patches of grass. When we are tired of watching, we dig the earth deep, seven pairs of holes in the ground, and one large one on each end of the seven pairs. We take turns tossing our pebbles into the holes. We remove the pebbles, also taking turns. We capture more and more of them until one of us wins. The game begins again.

The sounds of car engines mix with the sounds of the crickets. It is late evening, and the sky is grey. Car headlights sneak through the spaces between the metal rods of the gate. The grey becomes a little less grey, a little like day. Still, mosquitoes swirl around, and I swat at them, and I swat at myself, and Eno stops with the game, unties one of the two wrappers from around her waist, hands it to me.

At the clothesline, Ekaite is slapping too. She is slapping even more than Eno and I. Her skirt only comes down to her knees; she is not wearing a wrapper with which she can cover her legs.

I say, 'They bite us all the same.'

Eno says, 'No, they bite Ekaite more. Even the mosquitoes prefer fair skin.' The words come out in a mutter. Her tone is something between anger and dejection. I imagine the flesh of a ripe pawpaw. It is not quite the shade of Ekaite's skin, but it, too, is fair. I throw Eno's wrapper over my legs.

Emmanuel walks by, carrying a bucket. Water trickles down the sides of the bucket. He stops by Ekaite, and his lips curve into a crooked smile. Then maybe they share a joke, because soon comes the cracking of his laughter, and then hers, surging, rising, then tapering into the night sounds, at the very moment when it seems that their laughter might become insufferable. I look at Eno. Eno frowns.

Emmanuel pours the water out of the bucket, at the corner of the compound where the sand dips into the earth like a sewer. The scent of chlorine billows in the air, and I think of Onyechi and her swearing. I exhume the memory of the morning break, toss it about in my mind, like a pebble in the air, as if to get a feel for its texture, its potential, its capacity for success. And then I tell it to Eno.

When the sky grows black, I hand Eno back her wrapper, and we go into the house. We cut through the kitchen, pass the dining room, head down the corridor, and enter together into the bathroom. Papa and Mama do not catch us. They are closed off in their room.

In the bathroom, we first pour the bleach into the bucket, only a quarter of the way full. Then we watch the water bubble out of the faucet. We inhale and exhale deeply, and the sound of our breathing is weirdly louder than the sound of the running water. We caress the bucket with our eyes as if we are caressing our very hearts. The bucket fills. We turn the faucet off and gaze into the bucket. We are still gazing when Ekaite calls Eno. Her voice booms down the corridor, and Eno runs off quickly to answer, more quickly than usual because she knows well that she should not be in the bathroom with me. Because Eno knows that she must instead use the housegirls' bathroom, outside in the housegirls' quarters in the far corner of the backyard. But mostly, when Ekaite calls, Eno runs off quickly, because dinner will be served in just an hour, and Eno will have to help in its preparation.

★

At the dining table, Papa sits at the head, Mama by his side. The scent of egusi soup enters through the kitchen. Mama picks up her spoon, looks into it, unscrews the tiny canister, still with the spoon in her hand. It is lavender, the canister. The lipstick in it is a rich colour, red like the hibiscus flower; and it rises from the container slowly, steadily, like a lizard cautiously peeking out of a hole. Overhead the ceiling fan rattles and buzzes. The air conditioner hums, like soft snoring. In the kitchen we hear the clang-clanging of Ekaite's and Eno's food preparation: of the pestle hitting the mortar, yam being pounded for the soup. Off and on, there is the sound of the running faucet. We listen to the clink of silverware on glass. I imagine the plates and utensils being set out on the granite countertop, and then I hear a sound like the shutting of the fridge, that shiny, stainless-steel door all the way from America. And I wonder if Ekaite ever takes the time to look at her reflection in the door. And if she does, does she see herself in that superior way in which I imagine all fair people see themselves?

A bowl of velvet tamarinds sits at the centre of the table. It is a glass bowl in the shape of a dissected apple, and its short glass stem leads to a small glass leaf. Mama bought the bowl on one of her business trips overseas. She returned from that trip with other things too – silk blouses from Macy's, some Chanel, bebe, Coach, some Nike apparel. The evening she returned, she tossed all the items in piles on her side of the bed. She tossed herself contentedly, too, on the bed, on a small area on Papa's side, the only remaining space. She held up some of the overseas items for me to see. One blouse she lifted up closer to me, held it to my chest. It was the yellow of a ripe pineapple. 'Will lighten you up,' she said. She threw it to me. I didn't reach for it in time. It dropped to the floor.

The first magazine arrived two weeks later, *Cosmopolitan*, pale faces and pink lips decorating the cover, women with hair the colour of fresh corn. Perfect arches above their eyes.

Next was *Glamour*, then *Elle*. And every evening following that, Mama would sit on the parlour sofa for hours, flipping through the pages of the magazines, her eyes moving rapidly over and over the same pages, as if she were studying hard for the fashion equivalent of the university entrance exams.

I stare at the dissected apple, at the velvet tamarinds in it. I imagine picking one of the tamarinds up, a small one, something smaller than those old kobo coins, smaller than the tiniest one of them. Ekaite shuffles into the dining room, Eno close behind. They find themselves some space between me and the empty chair next to me. Ekaite sets the first tray down, three bowls of pounded yam.

She lifts the first bowl out of the tray, setting it on the placemat in front of Mama. Mama smiles at her, thanks her. Then, 'Osiso, osiso,' Mama says. 'Quick, quick, bring the soup!' Ekaite hurries back to where Eno is standing, takes out a bowl of soup from Eno's tray, sets it in front of Mama. Mama says, 'Good girl. Very good girl.' The skin around Mama's eyes wrinkles from her deepening smile. Ekaite nods but does not smile back. Eno, by my side, is more than unsmiling, and I can hardly blame her. But then I remember the bucket in the bathroom, and I feel hope billowing in me. Hope rising: the promise of relief.

It is Eno who serves Papa and me our food. She puts our dishes of pounded yam and soup on our placemats, still unsmiling. Papa thanks her, but it is a thank you that lacks all the fawning of Mama's to Ekaite. He thanks her in his quiet, aloof way, as if his mind is in his office, or somewhere far from home.

Mama waves Eno away. I watch her hand waving, the gold rings on her fingers, the bracelet that dangles from her wrist.

'Uzoamaka,' Mama says, when Eno and Ekaite have disappeared into the kitchen. 'You are looking very tattered today.'

Papa squints at her. I don't respond.

'It's no way to present yourself at the dinner table,' she says. The words tumble out of her mouth, one connected to the other, and I imagine rolls of her pounded yam all lined up on her plate, no space between them. Like her words, I think, that American way, one word tumbling into the next with no space between.

Papa looks at me for a moment, taking me in as if for the first time in a long time. 'How was school today?' he asks.

'Fine,' I say.

Mama says, 'A good week so far. A good month even. Imagine, an entire month and no strike! Surprising, with the way those lecturers are always on strike.'

'No, no strike so far,' I say.

'In any case,' Mama says. 'Not to worry.' She pauses. 'Arrangements are already being made.'

Papa shakes his head slightly, barely perceptibly, but we both see, Mama and I.

'She needs a good education,' Mama says to him, as if to counter the shaking of his head. She turns to me. 'You need a good education,' she says to me. It is not a new idea, this one of a good education, but she has that serious look on her face, as if she is weighing it with the thoughtfulness that accompanies new ideas. 'That is what America will give you,' she says. 'A solid education. And no strikes. Imagine, with a degree from America, you can land a job with a big company here, or maybe even remain in America. Land of opportunities.' She smiles at me. Her smile is wide.

Papa stuffs a roll of soup-covered pounded yam into his mouth. He keeps his eyes on me. Mama turns back to her food. She rolls her pounded yam, dips it into the bowl of soup, swallows. For a while, no-one speaks.

'In the meantime, you can't walk around looking tattered the way you do, shirt untucked, hair unbrushed. As for your face, you'd do well to dab some powder on. It will help brighten you up.'

Papa clears his throat. Mama turns to look at him. His eyes narrow at her. She starts to speak, but her words trail into a murmur and then into nothing at all.

There is another silence. This time it is Mama who clears her throat. Then she turns to me. She says, 'Even Ekaite presents herself better than you do. The bottom line is that you could learn a little something from her. Housegirl or not.'

I roll my eyes and feel the heat rising in my cheeks.

'Very well mannered, that one. Takes care of herself. Beautiful all around.' It is not the first time she is saying this.

I roll my eyes again, and then, 'Eno is pretty too,' I say. It is the first time that I am countering Mama on this. I only intend to mutter it, but it comes out louder than a mutter. I look up to find Mama glaring at me. Papa's eyes are also on me; they are just a little sharper than before.

'Eno is pretty too,' Mama repeats, sing-songy, mockingly. 'Foolish Eno. Dummy Eno.' She has to say 'dummy' twice, because the first time it comes out too Nigerian, with the accent on the last syllable instead of on the first. She tells me that Eno is no comparison to Ekaite. Not just where beauty is concerned. What a good housegirl Ekaite is, she says. She adds, an unnecessary reminder, that when Ekaite was around Eno's age, which is to say fourteen, the same age as me, Ekaite already knew how to make egusi and okra soup. And what tasty soups

Ekaite made! Even Ekaite's beans and yams, Mama continues, were the beans and yams of an expert, at fourteen. 'The girl knows how to cook,' she concludes. 'Just a good girl all around.' She pauses. 'Eno is no comparison. No comparison at all.'

Papa clears his throat. 'They're both good girls,' he says. He nods at me, smiles, a weak smile. In that brief moment I wonder what he knows. Whether he knows, like I do, that it's only bias, the way Mama feels about Ekaite. Whether he knows, like I do, that the reason for the bias is that Ekaite's face reminds her of the faces she sees on her magazines from abroad. Because, of course, Ekaite's complexion is light and her nose is not as wide and her lips not as thick as mine or Eno's. I look at him and I wonder if he knows, like I do, that Mama doesn't go as far as saying these last bits because, of course, she'd feel a little shame in saying it.

He dips his pounded yam into his soup. Mama does the same.

I don't touch my food. Instead, I stare at the velvet tamarinds, and I remember the first time she came back with boxes of those creams. Esoterica, Movate, Skin Success, Ambi. It was around the time the television commercials started advertising them – the fade creams. And we'd go to the Everyday Emporium, and there'd be stacks of them at the entrance, neat pyramids of creams. It was around this time too that the first set of girls in school started to grow lighter. Mama's friends, the darker ones, started to grow lighter, too. Mama did not at first grow light with them. She was cautious. She'd only grow light if she had the best-quality creams, not just the brands they sold at the Everyday Emporium. She wanted first-rate, the kinds she knew America would have. And so she made the trip and returned with boxes of creams.

Movate worked immediately for her. In just a few weeks, her skin had turned that shade of yellow. It worked for her knuckles, for her knees. Yellow all around, a uniform yellow, almost as bright as Ekaite's pawpaw skin.

She insisted I use the cream too. With Movate, patches formed all over my skin, dark and light patches, like shadows on a wall. She insisted I stop. People would know, she said. Those dark knuckles and kneecaps and eyelids. People would surely know. We tried Esoterica next. A six-month regimen. Three times a day. No progress at all. Skin Success was no success. Same with Ambi. 'Not to worry,' Mama said. 'They're always coming up with new products in America. Soon enough we'll find something that works.'

We must have been on Ambi the day Ekaite walked in on us – into my bedroom, not thinking that I was there. I should have been at school. She was carrying a pile of my clothes, washed and dried and folded for me.

Ekaite looked at the containers of creams on my bed.

Mama chuckled uncomfortably. 'Oya ga-wa,' she said. Well, go ahead.

Ekaite walked to my dresser. The drawers slid open and closed. Empty-handed now, she walked back towards the door.

Mama chuckled again and said, 'Uzoamaka here will soon be fair like you.'

Ekaite nodded. 'Yes, Ma.' There was a confused look on her face.

Mama cleared her throat. 'Fair like me, too.'

Ekaite nodded again. Then she turned to Mama. 'Odi kwa mma otu odi.' She's fine the way she is.

Mama shook her head. 'Oya ga-wa! Osiso, osiso.'

The door clicked closed.

★

I tell Mama that I'm not feeling well. An upset stomach. I excuse myself from the table before she has a chance to respond.

I carry my dishes into the kitchen, where Eno is waiting for me. Ekaite sits on a stool close to the floor. I feel her eyes on me and on Eno.

Inside the bathroom, the air is humid and smells clean, purified, a chemical kind of fresh. There is no lock on the door, but we make sure to close it behind us.

Eno holds the towel and stands back, but I call her to me, because I am again finding myself sceptical of the water and of the bleach. In my imagination, I see Clara's suspicious eyes, and I hear Boma's disbelieving laugh. Fear catches me, and I think perhaps we should not bother, perhaps we should just pour everything out. But then I hear Mama's voice, saying, 'Foolish Eno. Dummy Eno.' I take the towel from Eno. 'You should go first,' I say. It is a deceitful reason that I give, but it is also true: 'Because you're not supposed to be here. That way you'll be already done by the time anyone comes to chase you out.'

Eno nods. She concedes straight away.

She gets on her knees, bends her body over the wall of the bathtub so that her upper half hangs horizontally above the tub, so that her face is just above the bucket.

'We'll do only the face today,' I say. 'Dip it in until you feel something like a tingle.'

She dips her face into the water. She stays that way for some time, holding her breath. Even if I'm not the one with my face submerged, it is hard for me to breathe. So much anticipation.

Eno lifts up her face. 'My back is starting to ache, and I don't feel anything.'

'You have to do it for longer,' I say. 'Stand up, stretch your back. But you have to try to stay longer.'

Eno stands up. She lifts her hands above her head in a stretch. She gets back down on her knees, places her face into the bucket again.

'Only get up when you feel the tingling,' I say.

Time passes.

'Do you feel it yet?'

The back of Eno's head moves from side to side, a shake with her face still in the water.

More time passes.

'Not yet?'

The back of Eno's head moves again from side to side.

'Okay. Come up.'

She lifts her face from the water first. She stands up. The colour of her skin seems softer to the eyes, just a little lighter than before. I smile at her. 'It's working,' I say. 'But we need to go full force.'

'Okay,' she says. 'Good.' She watches as I pour the liquid from the bucket into the tub. We both watch as the water drains; we listen as it gurgles down the pipe. I take the bucket out of the tub, place it in a corner of the bathroom by the sink. The bath bowl is sitting in the sink. I pick it up, hold it above the tub, pour the bleach straight into it. I get down on my knees, call Eno to my side, tell her to place her face into the bowl. She does.

Only a little time passes, and then she screams, and her scream fills the bathroom, saturates every tiny bit of the room, and I am dizzy with it. Then there is the thud and splash of the bowl in the tub, then there is the thud of the door slamming into the wall. Ekaite rushes towards us, sees that it is Eno who is in pain. She reaches her hands out to Eno, holds Eno's face in her palms. Eno screams, twists her face. Her cheeks contort as if she is sucking in air. She screams and screams. I feel the pain in my own face. Ekaite looks as if she feels it too, and for a moment I think I see tears forming in her eyes. Papa looms in the doorway, then enters the bathroom. He looks fiercely at me. He asks, 'What did you do to her? What did you do?' In the doorway, I see Mama just watching, her eyes flicking this way and that.

'What did you do?' Papa asks again. I turn to him, pleading, wanting desperately to make my case, but I don't find the words. I turn to Mama. I beg her to explain. She looks blankly at me, a little confusion in her eyes. I stand in the middle of them, frozen with something like fear, something not quite guilt.

By then, even Emmanuel has made his way into the house, abandoning his post at the gate. He stands just behind Mama, and his peering eyes seem to ask me that same question: *What did you do?*

My legs feel weak. I turn to Eno, I smile at her. I think of Mama and her creams. 'Don't worry,' I say. 'We'll find something that works.' Eno continues to scream. I blink my eyes as if to blink myself awake.

Days later, when the scabs start to form, I imagine peeling them off like the hard shell of a velvet tamarind. Eno's flesh underneath the scabs is the reddish-yellow of the tamarind's pulp, not quite the yellow of a ripe pawpaw peel. And even if I know that this scabby fairness of hers is borne of injury, a temporary fairness of skinless flesh, patchy, and ugly in its patchiness, I think how close she has come to having skin like Onyechi's, and I feel something like envy in me, because what she has wound up with *is* fairness after all. Fairness, if only for a while.

Story, Story!

It was a story that Nneoma had told three times before, each time in the church on Rumuola Road. The church was not the same one that she attended as a child – not that small one out in the village, with hardly more than a dozen benches in it. Not that old one where she used to sit, a long time ago, worshipping alongside her parents. (Her parents had hoped that she'd one day get married in that village church, but it was now evident that Nneoma's was a life that refused to converge with hopes. Her only consolation was that at least she'd tried. This failure of her life to merge with her parents' hopes, of it to merge with even her own hopes, was clearly not any fault of hers. She reasoned it this way, as if that settled it.)

The church was round and two storeys high. Just like a wedding cake, Nneoma often thought. It was true: just like a wedding cake, its top layer was a smaller circle than its bottom. And the two cases of stairs that ran along the exterior walls, connecting the top and bottom storeys, were a little like the cake's decoration. Icing in the shape of stairs.

Being a city church, it was large. Inside the main hall, benches stood in circular formation so that they appeared to radiate from the middle, like a wave whose centre was the pulpit. Here and there, between the benches, metal floor fans also stood, oscillating and buzzing negligibly from their posts. Even with the fans, it was warm inside the church.

It was on those benches, and in that warmth, that Nneoma told the story. She told it in bits, in the breaks before and after and during the service. She made sure to tell it only to visiting women, because the sudden absence of a regular member would surely be noted by the pastor, and by the congregation as a whole.

The last time she told the story – two and a half, nearly three years ago – it was to a visiting woman that she told it. The woman was very pretty, with high cheekbones, much like Nneoma's own. The woman had sharp, penetrating eyes: she might have suspected all along. Or perhaps she had not suspected. Perhaps she was just that kind of woman: sharp, but merely on the superficial level – sharp eyes, sharp jaw, a very sharp fashion sense.

The woman was wearing red lipstick and gold earrings, a nice lace blouse and bangles that dangled up and down her wrists. She had painted a mole on her face, just above her lips, with the same black pencil that she used to line her lips – at least Nneoma suspected as much. It was the fashion, Nneoma knew. A mole, but some called it a beauty mark.

The other two women to whom Nneoma told the story were not pretty women, but rather ugly ones who wore no earrings, no lipstick, no beauty marks. The telling of the story to these two women had occurred on separate instances, of course – there had been at least a four-year gap in between.

In any case, both of these women wore plain blouses – not made of lace; and both of them were even a little foul-smelling, something like the scent of rotten fruit. It was as if they had given up altogether, this refusal of theirs even to feign beauty. Perhaps it was a mockery of beauty, Nneoma thought. All the same, she told them the story.

Nneoma would continue to tell the story. She was after all the one who found Ezioma that day. Ezioma, lying on the bed in her yellow nightgown, the blanket pulled up to her chest.

Ezioma, eyes closed, sleeping as peacefully as ever. And the baby in her womb, sleeping as peacefully as her.

Sunday had come again. Nneoma was once more in the church on Rumuola Road. She made her way to her usual seat, in the second storey of the church – on one of the benches farthest away from the pulpit. The sun was coming in through the windows, laying itself in long, tapering streaks on the floor. Nneoma sat, mindlessly observing the streaks of light.

The hall filled up so that there were only a few spaces left to sit, most of them on those benches along the perimeter. These were usually the last to fill.

When the woman approached, taking a seat on Nneoma's bench, Nneoma felt her presence but did not at first lift her gaze. Nearby, a fan rattled and buzzed, its metal frame glimmering where the sun landed on it.

The woman greeted Nneoma good morning, and only as Nneoma turned to greet the woman back did she look up to see the woman's face. In those brief moments she observed that the woman was new to the church. She observed that the woman's eyes appeared tired. She observed the beads of sweat on the woman's forehead. Her eyes fell to the woman's protruding belly. She observed that the woman was with child. What luck, she thought, as she reached into her handbag to take out the handkerchief in it. She offered the handkerchief to the woman. 'Were akwa,' she said. Take the cloth. The woman accepted.

Nneoma allowed her eyes to fall on the woman's belly once more, to settle there long enough for the woman to become aware of her gaze.

'Iwere umu nke gi?' the woman asked.

Nneoma shook her head. No, she said. She did not have any children of her own.

The woman nodded sympathetically. All around them people chatted; voices rose.

A long time ago, when she was just beginning at Staff School (she was twenty-four at the time and had just finished her Youth Service), Nneoma had the impression that she would marry. Because Obinna – Mr Nkangineme – the headmaster, had kept his eyes on her. He had been more watchful of her than of any of the other teachers, even more watchful of her than of Ezioma, who had started at the school at the same time as Nneoma.

Before Obinna, no other man had shown interest in Nneoma. She was, after all, shy and socially awkward. She could no more hold a conversation than a gaze. Not to mention that she did not fill out her dresses the way many other girls did. But even when she began to fill them out, it appeared it was already too late. It seemed the boys had grown accustomed to paying her no attention; they continued that way throughout secondary school, throughout her years at the university, even throughout her Youth Service. She watched as the other girls put on their lipstick, as they fussed with their dresses and hair, as they went out fervently on dates.

But Obinna gave her hope. He would sometimes come into her class after school was dismissed, taking a seat across from her, facing her. Sometimes he leaned into the back of his chair.

The first time he came, Nneoma was rummaging through the drawer of her desk. There was a scent of dead roaches coming from the drawer, and so she had lowered her head into the drawer to see if she could find the roaches. It was conceivable that they'd be there – the desk was old, its wood chipped at the edges, with bite marks where mice appeared to have gnawed at it.

Opposite her desk was a large window. Sometimes, while the children worked silently in their notebooks, she gazed at a vanishing point somewhere beyond the window, beyond the orange and guava and plantain trees, whose leaves sometimes rustled in the morning or afternoon breeze. She looked beyond the patchy field of green and yellow grass, beyond the tombstones in the cemetery across the school compound. She'd fade away into mindless thoughts, thoughts which dissolved the instant any student made a sound.

Well, even with the window, she did not see him coming, not because of her distant daydreaming, but rather because she was so immersed in her search for the dead roaches. He startled her, and she gasped. Then she chuckled softly, embarrassed by her fright. He asked if he could help her find what she was looking for. She straightened up, smiled politely at him. He was wearing a taupe coloured agbada trimmed with gold. His hair was not so grey then. He held a hat in his hand, fussing with it as he made his way towards her desk. He brought with him a sweet smell, the scent of plantain leaves warmed by sunlight.

The chair on the other side of her desk was where students sometimes sat when she called them to have a one-on-one conference with her. He shook her hand first, then sat on the chair, leaned into the back of the seat, as if to create more space between them.

'Are you settling fine?' he asked.

She nodded.

'Be sure to let me know if you need anything – chalk, paper, pens and pencils. Any supplies.'

She nodded. 'Thank you,' she said.

He stayed for just a moment more and then he rose from the seat, made his way back out of the door.

This was how that first meeting went. He might have done

the same with Ezioma, and in fact with all four of the new teachers who had gained employment at Staff School that year. He might have gone to their classes and offered chalk, paper, pens and pencils. And before all of that, he might have shaken their hands too. But Nneoma suspected that he didn't. She was sure he'd taken those extra steps just for her.

All around them, in the church, the voices quieted down. Nneoma leaned over to the woman. 'The pastor will soon begin,' she explained.

The woman nodded.

'But don't worry, we still have a few minutes before he does. We can talk for a bit.' She looked at the woman's belly once more. 'How far?' she asked.

'Seven months, almost eight. Counting down the weeks now.'

Nneoma smiled. 'I had a friend,' she said. 'Ezioma.' She fussed with her hands, which rested on her handbag. She tangled and untangled her fingers. There was a silence.

The woman cleared her throat. 'Your friend,' she said. 'She was pregnant, too?'

Nneoma smiled gratefully. She nodded. 'Yes, she was pregnant. She used to come to this church.'

The woman nodded, as if to signal Nneoma to continue.

Nneoma paused thoughtfully. Then she said, 'You know, here the pastor tells us to greet one another, and we do – by shaking hands, you know. We used to hug, but one day he told us to stop. Only to shake hands. Because he was afraid that all the hugging and embracing was scaring off the visitors. Makes sense. I suppose it can be a scary thing to have to hug a stranger.'

This time it was the woman who appeared thoughtful.

Nneoma watched her. 'Yes, hand-shaking seems a good enough greeting,' the woman said.

'Ezioma thought so too,' Nneoma said.

By now the pastor had climbed onto the stage. He looked small in the distance, but Nneoma noticed when he raised his hand and tapped the microphone, the way he did every Sunday – to check that it was working. He tapped once, twice. The sound of the tapping was like the static on a radio.

'This is the day the Lord has made,' he said. 'Let us rejoice and be glad in it!' His voice was strong and convincing in its strength. It caused Nneoma to feel uplifted and hopeful – the way it always did.

The pastor instructed them to greet one another. They stood up to do so, shaking hands, just as Nneoma had explained. The pastor then retreated to the corner of the stage. The liturgist replaced him at the microphone, motioning everyone to rise for the call to confession. Everyone rose.

The liturgist was wearing a white dress shirt, no tie, black trousers. He said, 'If we say we have no sin, we deceive ourselves, and the truth is not in us. If we confess our sins, He Who is faithful and just will forgive us and cleanse us from all unrighteousness.'

A murmur arose – quiet, harmonized prayers. Nneoma felt the tears well up in her eyes. She was penitent, and wished she could stop with her sins.

The liturgist concluded with the prayer of confession. Nneoma swiftly wiped her eyes.

The pastor made his way back to the podium. There, he stood flipping through the sheets of his sermon. As he flipped, Nneoma leaned over to the woman. 'I found her in her bed,' Nneoma said. 'Just sleeping like a baby.'

'Who?'

'Ezioma,' Nneoma said. 'It's been years now, but the memory is still so fresh.'

'Sorry,' the woman replied, sympathetically.

Nneoma nodded.

'And the baby?'

'Gone with her,' Nneoma said, shaking her head now. She felt the tears forming in her eyes, and soon she was wiping them away with her hands. The woman just watched her; Nneoma could feel her watchful eyes. Then she could feel the woman's hand on her, as the woman reached out to pat her gently on the arm.

Nneoma remembered Ezioma then. She remembered that it was at this specific moment of the service, all those years ago, that she invited Ezioma over for lunch. Ezioma had been married a year by then. Her husband was a contractor for Shell and was out of town on business. Not that he ever attended church, but on a normal Sunday he would have been home, and Ezioma would have had to return home to him.

Well, that Sunday, Ezioma accepted the invitation.

In Nneoma's house, they talked about the sermon at church, about their problem students at Staff School, about the way they were getting along with other teachers. Nneoma would have brought up Obinna – Mr Nkangineme – but she knew it was better to keep him to herself – her own little secret.

They talked about the baby Ezioma was carrying and about Ezioma's husband – Ezioma gushed about how lucky she was to have him for a husband, about how good he had been to her, and how much more so she knew he would be to the child.

It was painful for Nneoma to discuss Ezioma's husband and baby. If she had been married herself, and with a child on the way, this would have been different. Well, she consoled herself with the thought that at least her work at Staff School allowed her the opportunity to play a motherly role. It was hardly a consolation, though, because there were of course the after-school hours to contend with. Those terrible hours when she found herself alone again. Alone, but with all that longing. Sometimes the longing became physical, like hunger pangs. She could feel it within the walls of her stomach, and sometimes it was so intense that it caused her to lash out and strike any nearby objects. She overturned stacks of student papers, only to settle back down and then face the tedious task of reorganizing them. She threw dishes into the walls, only to have to clean up the shattered glass. Sometimes the longing caused her to pull angrily at her hair, or to beat herself – her arms, her thighs – striking and striking until she was too worn out to continue. Sometimes she simply wailed.

It was as a result of this longing that Nneoma prepared well for her lunch with Ezioma. Before the lunch, she had even taken the bus all the way to the village of Ogbigbo, so that she could visit the dibia there, so that the dibia could tell her how to go about the transaction with Ezioma in the best way possible. After her visit with the dibia, Nneoma had returned home and prepared the lunch, all to the dibia's specifications. She made some jolloff rice with chicken, and some ogbono soup with garri. Both of these were main dishes, but Nneoma prepared them nevertheless, so that Ezioma could have her choice.

They ate sitting on the chairs that Nneoma had set out on her veranda. It would be more relaxed that way, the dibia had said. And so, of course, Nneoma complied.

The pastor was speaking now, having finally begun his sermon. Still, Nneoma continued her conversation with the woman. She spoke in a hushed voice.

'Di-gi, o no ebe?' she asked.

'Home,' the woman replied, also in a hushed voice, and keeping her eyes in the direction of the pastor. 'He's at home putting together furniture. Arranging the house. We're still unpacking. But by next week, we should be settled, and then he'll join me in church.'

Nneoma nodded. 'It's good to have a husband,' she said. 'Makes things easier.'

The woman looked at Nneoma now, she let out a quiet laugh, but she nodded, too. 'Yes,' she said. 'Some things it does make easier.' She turned back from Nneoma and looked once more in the direction of the pastor, who still stood at the podium delivering his sermon.

Nneoma resigned herself to her thoughts, while the woman appeared to resign herself to the sermon.

Nneoma thought of Obinna, of those years when she was sure that he'd be the one. She was not quite sure how things could have gone so wrong. She remembered the day they did.

That day, he had come into her classroom again.

He was wearing a button-down shirt, tucked into his trousers. A tie hung down from his neck. She was just sitting at her desk, gazing out the window. As had become his habit, he came in and took that same chair on the other side of her desk.

He'd brought with him a box of chalk and a blackboard eraser. 'This should do for the next few weeks,' he said. 'But let me know if you need more.'

She nodded. She allowed her fingers to touch and linger on his as she accepted the package. He eyed her quizzically. She noticed this, was flattered by it. How wonderful, she thought, the way he seemed to caress her face with his eyes.

Now, when she thought of it, she knew that there were things she should have considered before going ahead with her plan. Practical things, like, was he in fact interested in her? Was he just performing a duty, just handing out supplies so that his school would run smoothly?

But it had not even occurred to her to question his affection.

She accepted the box of chalk along with the eraser and placed them on her desk. She looked at him – at his hair, his face, his eyes. His hair appeared greyer now, but his face retained its youth. His teeth were crooked, but in a way she found endearing.

She took in all of his features as he stood in front of her, continued to take in all of it as he asked, 'Is there anything else I can do for you?'

She shook her head.

He nodded and then turned to leave. Just as he turned, she shouted, 'Wait!' It came out like a gasp.

He turned back around.

She was giddy with anticipation. It occurred to her that soon she would be able to make the announcement to her mama, to her papa, to everyone who mocked, who doubted. She would be able to say, 'I'm getting married.' Or, 'Here is my husband-to-be.' And she would present Obinna to them.

She was wearing two wrappers, both tied at her waist. There were concentric designs on the wrappers – circles and spheres of different sizes, clusters of them meeting at the middle. The blouse she wore that day was made of lace and was short-sleeved, with a low neckline that came just below her shoulders.

She had secured the hem of the blouse to the wrappers with safety pins. Also, she had made sure to tuck the hem of the longer wrapper – just the edge of it – beneath one of the legs of her desk.

She rose up from her seat then, abruptly. She felt the tug

of the desk's leg on her wrapper, and the wrapper's tug on her blouse. The wrapper slid down her waist, still covering her body, but it pulled the blouse with it further down below her shoulders so that it exposed half of her chest, that smooth yellow-brownness of it, smooth but not flat, because there was of course the matter of the exposed breast, which was small but round and full, which rose and tapered into a nipple the colour of lumber wood. The nipple was nearly a perfect circle, she knew, and at the very tip of it – at the very tip of the other one, too – was that tiny opening, from which she desperately hoped that milk would one day flow, enough to nourish her child.

Obinna gasped then. 'Miss Enwere!' he exclaimed. 'Cover yourself!'

Nneoma stood where she was, just looking at him.

'Miss Enwere! Do you hear me?'

Finally she said, 'Obinna, don't worry. Everything is just the way it should be.' She pulled the wrapper from underneath the leg of the desk then. She held it – held the portion that she had latched on to as she pulled. She walked over to him. Her blouse still hung down her chest.

When she reached him, she took his hand in hers, placed it on her chest, just above her exposed breast. She sighed with satisfaction. There was release, a blissful lightness in the mere touch of his skin on hers. She breathed deeply.

'I want this,' she said. 'I want *you*. Don't you want me, too?' Why had she even asked this last question? At the time, she was sure he wanted her too.

He jerked his hand away, his face angry. She did not understand.

'Obinna,' she said. It was both an exclamation and a question.

'Pull yourself together, Miss Enwere!' he said. 'Do you value your job? *Do you value your job?!* I suggest you pull yourself together, or you will soon be out of a job!' He turned to leave the room. At the door, he stopped. 'And, from now on,' he said, 'it's Mr Nkangineme to you.'

For months afterwards, it was an embarrassment to see him, even from a distance — at morning assemblies, especially. He stopped coming to her classroom to drop off supplies. Or, rather, he must have dropped them off late in the evenings after she was gone for the day, or early in the mornings before she arrived. But he was a professional, and she knew that word of the incident had not spread from him. She was thankful for that.

Months passed, and she remained at the school, because she had been unsuccessful in finding other work. Eventually, it seemed he forgot the incident and began again to bring her supplies. They remained professional about those brief encounters. She called him Mr Nkangineme.

Now the pastor called for silent prayer, and the church was quiet for a minute or two. The pastor finished with the Lord's Prayer, first in Igbo, then in English. The congregation recited along with him, their voices loud and imploring.

Next, the choir began to sing, and the ushers came around carrying circular golden trays in which the tithe money was placed. When the tray arrived at her, Nneoma dug into her handbag and placed her money on the tray, more than a few naira bills, in multiples of a hundred, more than enough to buy a loaf of bread. The woman next to her dug into her purse as well; Nneoma watched. The woman placed some naira bills into the tray. Nneoma smiled approvingly at her as she did. The woman smiled back.

When all the money had been collected, the ushers gathered in front of the stage. The pastor moved forward to collect each tray. The choir sang even louder now. *Praise God from Whom all blessings flow. Praise Him, all creatures here below* . . .

When the singing was done, the pastor delivered his closing address. 'Go in peace,' he said to the congregation. 'Return no-one evil for evil. And in all things, seek the good.'

The choir sang briefly, just a refrain. Members of the congregation began to rise, their voices along with their bodies. The service was over.

Nneoma turned to the woman. 'My friend Ezioma,' she said. 'I met her at work. I teach at Staff School, in Abuloma.'

The woman nodded, picking up her handbag from her lap and making to rise.

'It was thanks to my invitation that she ever even started to come to this church. I invited her, you see.'

'I see,' the woman said, nodding.

Nneoma skipped the part about the dibia and the potion. She jumped to the lunch. She told the woman again that Ezioma was pregnant and showing by that time. Eight months, just like the woman. Perhaps Ezioma had eaten too much that day, Nneoma told the woman. Because the next day, Monday, she did not show up to school. On Tuesday, she did not show up again. On Wednesday, Mr Nkangineme held a teachers' meeting early, at 7 a.m., an hour and a half before the students arrived. All the teachers gathered, sat around that long oval table in the headmaster's office. He had been unable to contact Ezioma by phone, Nneoma told the woman. And Ezioma's husband was apparently still away on the work trip. Mr Nkangineme had called the meeting to see if any of the teachers had heard from Ezioma.

By now the woman was no longer making to leave. She had settled back into the bench, taken with Nneoma's story.

Nneoma continued.

Perhaps she was ill, Mr Nkangineme had speculated. Maybe too ill to contact the school. One of them should pay her a visit, to let her know that she was on their minds, in their prayers, he concluded.

But it should be someone who knew her well, he said. All the teachers agreed.

Who was closest to her then? the headmaster asked.

Eyes scanned the room. Most of them landed on Nneoma. By then, the teachers knew that Ezioma and Nneoma had grown close, that they sometimes walked home together after school. They'd heard that Ezioma sometimes attended church services with Nneoma on Rumuola Road.

Nneoma complied hesitantly. She asked the teachers when they thought was a good time for her to go.

The teachers responded that she should go as soon as possible. 'Now,' they said.

The gate to Ezioma's house was locked. There was no gateman, at least not at the time Nneoma arrived. She was forced to get on the tips of her toes. Then she reached inside the gate with her hands, manipulated the latch until she managed to open it. Lucky for her that there was no padlock.

She walked across the front yard, towards the front entrance. The door was wide – a double-leaf door – made of glass on the top half, wood on the bottom.

She knocked. Her heart had begun to beat fast by then. She could feel her palms sweating. She continued to knock, each one louder than the one before. She turned the knob as she knocked, but the door was locked. She shook it frantically. Eventually, it occurred to her to try to pick the lock. She reached for her hair, took out one of the bobby pins that held her hair in a bun. She inserted it this way and that, inside the key hole, to the side of the door where the bolt and socket met.

Finally, the door opened. Her heart beat even faster. In the parlour, everything was calm, except for the buzzing of the ceiling fan. But the air smelled moist, musty. When she breathed deeply enough, there was something in it like rotten soup.

A picture of Ezioma and her husband hung on another wall, smiling faces. In the picture, her husband wore a light-green agbada and sokoto. He had the look of an Oga, which perhaps he was, all that travelling he did. But there had been no gatemen guarding the gate, like big men often had. And there were no housegirls to be seen. In fact, the house itself was modest at best. But no matter, Nneoma thought. She turned from the picture to tackle the matter for which she had come.

There were two doors, one on each side of the corridor. There was a third door straight ahead. None of the doors was quite pulled closed. She pushed the one ahead first. She saw the toilet, a sink, the bath stall. Some towels hanging on a rack. She pulled the door back – not all the way closed, but just the way it had been.

She turned to her left. She pushed that door slowly. She felt her breath catch as it opened. What if things were exactly the way she expected they'd be? She'd cry, she thought. She'd cry for poor Ezioma. But she'd be grateful to the dibia. And she'd be grateful for the baby.

She entered the room. She could see a lump on one side of the double bed. That scent of rotten soup was stronger now than before. She moved closer, went directly to the lump. She found Ezioma there, just lying down, her blanket pulled up to her chest.

Nneoma began to cry then. She flipped the blanket from Ezioma's chest. She touched Ezioma's belly. It was stiff. She bent her head to be closer, listening for signs of life in Ezioma's rigid belly. She could not have been sure, but somehow Nneoma knew then that the baby had not survived. She moaned. She imagined Ezioma being buried in that cemetery across from the Staff School compound. She imagined the baby being buried with her. It infuriated her, the thought. She pounded her fist into the mattress, narrowly missing Ezioma's body. Over and over again, she pounded. Then she curled into a ball at the side of the bed. She cried, but there was no-one to hear.

It was afternoon by the time Nneoma picked herself up from the floor. She wiped her eyes with the hem of her blouse, which had by then sneaked out from underneath her wrapper. She did not have to look for the phone. It was there, sitting on the bedside table, on the other side of the bed. She picked it up, dialled the school. Obinna picked up. Mr Nkangineme. She told him exactly how it was. Almost exactly, anyway. She told him of the way she had found Ezioma – still sleeping in bed, only more than sleeping: dead. She told him that she'd been in shock, that she'd been curled up, crying by Ezioma's side all this time.

'My God!' he exclaimed. Then, 'Miss Enwere, I'm so sorry for your loss.' His tone was sympathetic.

Now, in church, the pregnant woman listened, expressed her sympathy as Nneoma told the story.

As she did with Mr Nkangineme, Nneoma left out any mention of her role in all of it – no mention of her visits to the dibia, no mention of the dibia's potion, or of its use in the preparation of the food she served Ezioma that Sunday lunch long ago. She did not tell the woman that part of her devastation about the situation was in the knowledge that she had sacrificed Ezioma but had wound up with no child after all.

What she did tell the woman was that all of this happened over a decade ago. Twelve years, to be exact. She was twenty-eight years old at the time.

'I'm sorry,' the woman said now, moving to embrace Nneoma. 'Ndo.' She repeated it, whispered it. Sorry.

For a moment, Nneoma remembered the pastor, his ban on hugs. She thought that perhaps the pastor was wrong. Perhaps hugs did nothing to scare the visitors away. Well, ban or not, here she was being embraced by this visitor. How she had missed these embraces! How long had it been since the last time someone held her this way? Very long – in fact, so long that she did not remember. She would savour it, then: she leaned into the embrace, grateful for it. She breathed in the musty scent of the woman. It was nourishing and comforting, the embrace.

Just as soon as the woman released her, Nneoma's thoughts were back to Ezioma again, and she remembered the days after she lost Ezioma and the baby, how she'd thought she heard people talking about her, gossiping about her being unmarried, about her being childless. Mgbaliga. Nwanyi–iga. 'Empty barrel. Old maid,' the voices said. She heard them as she walked down to the market, as she rode the bus on her errands, even in school she heard the whispers. The whispers scolded, ridiculed, condemned.

Her parents appeared to be whispering too, each time Nneoma stopped by to visit them in the village. They'd shake their heads disappointedly, and it seemed to her that they muttered something about how she would soon be past child-bearing age. It seemed to her that they muttered things like, 'All your friends are leaving you behind. Won't you do something about it?'

There, seated in the church beside the woman, Nneoma began to hear the voices again: Mgbaliga. Nwanyi-iga. MGBALIGA. NWANYI-IGA. She shook her head, trying to shake the voices away. To no avail. Then all the words of the day were mixing up in her head. Praise God. Confession. Nwanyi-iga. Sin. Creatures. Blessings. Di-gi, o no ebe? Mgbaliga!

She continued to shake her head, furiously now. Soon her thoughts were racing with the same things with which they raced around this period in her scheme: how happy she would be if it worked this time. How much she would love and nurture the child, never taking her eyes away from it. She would name the child Ekwutosina, if it were a girl. Cease your gossiping. An answer to those whispers. And, if it were a boy, Chukwuemeka. God has been very generous to me. Also an answer to the whispers.

'You should allow yourself to move on,' the woman said.

'Yes. I really should,' Nneoma replied emphatically. 'But it's hard.'

'What are you doing this evening?' the woman asked. 'You should drop by my house. All that with Ezioma was so long ago. You need to try to get over it. Come over. I'll prepare food. We'll eat. I will help you take your mind off it. We will talk of other things, get to know each other better. My husband will be busy working on the house. He won't disturb.'

Nneoma nodded, accepted. 'Da'lu. Imela,' she said. Thank you. 'What shall I bring?'

The woman waved her hand as if to say, *Don't worry about it.* 'Just bring yourself,' she said.

'Oh no, I must bring something,' Nneoma said. 'It wouldn't be right.'

The woman nodded. 'Okay,' she said. 'If you insist. Bring whatever you want.'

Nneoma nodded and thanked the woman again. Then she watched as the woman stood up finally to leave. The church was mostly cleared out now.

The woman paused. 'Are you all right?' she asked, her voice soft and concerned.

'Yes,' Nneoma replied. 'I will come this evening,' she said to the woman. But her mind was drifting again. She thought of the potion now. It had failed with Ezioma. It had failed with the women who came after Ezioma, all three of them. They had taken their babies along with them, just like Ezioma.

Suddenly Nneoma was doubtful. They were all such kind women, Nneoma thought. What sense was there in continuing to waste their lives like this?

She wondered if she should bother with this woman. No, she decided. She said it aloud: 'No!'

'Are you okay?' the woman asked again.

Nneoma grew even more doubtful. This doubt was not, had never been part of the plan. She rose from the bench. 'No,' she said to herself, softer now. 'Maybe I won't go after all.' Her intention now was to head out of the church – to walk in the direction of the nearest staircase, to go outside for fresh air. But beneath her the floor seemed to shake. She sat back down on the bench. Soon it appeared to her that the walls of the church were collapsing: a crumbling cake. She heard loud screaming and thuds of racing feet. She wanted to run too, but her legs refused to move. Her heart was beating fast, faster. It was a struggle to catch her breath. 'No more,' she said, very boldly. 'Not this evening. Not ever again.' But even as she said it, a part of her still hoped. It was a deep-seated hope borne of nothing more than habit. It was a desperate one, this hope. It was the hope that the woman would insist.

Runs Girl

The year Mama fell sick was the year Njideka confessed to me that she was a runs girl. I should have known. She walked around campus with shiny silk blouses hanging low on her shoulders, her stilettos making tiny dents in the earth. That year, the runs girls began to circulate the University of Port Harcourt campus. Or maybe they'd always been around. Maybe I only noticed them that year, with their expensive outfits and accessories – money written all over their bodies – because Mama was falling apart, and there was almost nothing I could do.

A bird had flown over our compound with a mouse in its mouth. A black bird, maybe a crow. From the parlour window, we watched it fly. It was lovely and surreal, like a painting. Beautiful blue skies as the backdrop to blackness and death.

The bird dropped the mouse on the ground within a few steps of our front door. We found it that evening, just before sunset. Its tail was twisted around its body, and its pelt was already stiff.

That evening, Mama snapped a branch off the guava tree in our backyard. She used the branch to pick up the mouse and to stick it in a plastic bag. I took the bag with me across the street, across the unpaved road, to the garbage dump there. I tossed the bag into the sea of trash.

Hours later, Mama began to feel sick. If Papa had still been alive, he would have chanted his usual saying: 'The witch cried yesterday; the child died today. Who does not know the cause of the child's death?'

But the doctors did not know. And even if they had known, chances are their diagnosis would have had nothing to do with the bird and the mouse. They were scientists, after all – not superstitious, like the rest of us.

It began with pain on the shoulder. Mama decided that for dinner we would have some goat meat in pepper soup, with more than the normal amount of utazi leaves. The leaves made the soup bitter. Mama said that the bitterness, in combination with the pepper, would chase the pain away.

But the next day she could barely move her left arm. We should have gone to the hospital straight away, but Mama said to hold off. They would charge us two thousand naira just to see the doctor. That was the amount they charged the last time we went, when Mama was having all those sweats, followed immediately by chills. That time, the doctors ran their tests and told her she was fine. Two thousand naira wasted and nothing fixed.

There was no telling that the doctors would solve the problem this time. Besides, Mama was certain it was the curse of the black bird – nothing a little praying and Bible reading couldn't fix, she said. So that second evening we read the Bible together, more fervently than ever.

NEPA had once again taken light away, but there was still a little glow from the sun coming in through the windows of our parlour, which was where we prayed every evening, kneeling on the tile floor, our bodies resting on the seat of the couch. *Happy is the man whom God correcteth: therefore despise not thou the chastening of the Almighty: For He maketh sore, and bindeth up: He woundeth, and His hands make whole. He shall deliver thee in six troubles: yea, in seven there shall no evil touch thee.* Her voice shook as she read. And the mosquitoes flew about the room, making soft whistling sounds near our ears. Mama must have found the sounds more irritating than usual, because suddenly she was no longer reading, and I was looking up to find her swatting the area around her head. And then she let out a piercing shriek: a sound I hope I never hear again for as long as I live.

When night finally came, Mama's moaning had still not stopped. Hours passed but there was no sleep for her, and no sleep for me. The pain was somewhere in her torso, she said, on the left side between the upper shoulder and the lower back. She could feel it also in her front. Just as she would expect a heart attack to feel, except there was no indication that her heart was the part in which the crumbling was taking place. It seemed the heart would be just fine, she said. Yet I observed the signs; all of them were far from promising.

In the end it was I who forced her to go to the hospital. We walked out the door early the next morning, taking small steps, my hands fastened securely around her waist.

'Slower, Ada,' Mama said.

I tightened my grip on her. 'Ndo,' I said. Sorry.

We took a taxi to the teaching hospital, one of those three-wheeled keke napeps that looked like something in between a minivan and a motorcycle. The roads were riddled with pot-holes, and in the keke napep, small as it was, we felt every one of those holes. Each time the vehicle bounced, Mama let out a yelp. And then she'd look at me, her eyes repentant, as if she'd somehow misbehaved.

I should have consoled her more. I should have told her I loved her. But how? Aside from prayers and practical exchanges, we rarely even talked those days just before she fell ill. I was busy with my studies, and she was busy with the market. And so there were silences, as if we no longer valued spoken words, as if spoken words were gaudy finishes on a delicate piece of art, unnecessary distractions from the masterpiece, whose substance was more meaningfully experienced if left unornamented.

There was no longer the Mama who used to tie her scarves on my head, making bows or floral designs out of the tailpieces. No longer the Mama who used to take me on long strolls around the neighbourhood, buying me corn and native pear or roasted bole. Those days, she'd tell me jokes and we'd laugh out loud as if we were the only people in the world. Some nights, she'd even rub a little lipstick on my lips, and she'd take me to Papa and say, 'Look how beautiful our daughter is!' And Papa would say, 'She's beautiful even without all that lipstick.' Mama would nod. 'Of course,' she'd say. 'But every girl needs to learn how to put on lipstick.' And we'd laugh, and I'd dance around and pucker my lips at Papa. He'd smile and humour me, until I grew tired of the show.

That Mama disappeared soon after Papa died. Year after year, she had grown less gregarious. Her mind was always on the market; how we would make money from the crops she sold to pay for this and for that. Of course, I understood her worry. Papa had gone and left us to fend for ourselves in a world where it was hard for a woman to do so honestly.

If I had tried to tell her I loved her on our taxi ride that day, it would not have made things any better. I would not have even known how to say it. *Mama, I have something to say?* Or, *Mama, I'm not just saying this because you're sick. I really feel it. Do you feel it for me, too?* Or, simply, *Mama, I love you.* No matter how I said it, it would have felt contrived, because we no longer said such tender things. And so I remained silent, only patting her lap gently each time the pain caused her to cry out.

★

I sat on a chair in the corner of the examination room. The fan buzzed on the ceiling, and the fluorescent lights above were shining bright.

A bald-headed doctor entered the room. He took her blood pressure, which he reported was just fine. Then he unbuttoned her shirt, just enough so that he could take a look at her chest. Her skin was a light shade of brown, and it was easy to see that there was redness and swelling in the area around and below her left shoulder. And in the corner where her sternum met the clavicle, just beneath her neck, there was a bulge.

He tapped around those areas. Every time he tapped, she yelped.

'We'll have to run some tests,' the doctor said.

We walked down two sets of crowded hallways, descended two flights of concrete stairs, with flies buzzing, children crying and Mama moaning.

First they attached thin wires to her chest and arms with tape. Then the machine beeped and reported the results on a strip of pink graph paper: horizontal lines that peaked and dipped at regular intervals. Perhaps it was her heart after all, I thought. But the electrocardiogram results were normal. Her heart appeared fine.

Next were the X-rays. I waited outside while the nurse took Mama into the room. It was afternoon by the time the results came back. The fluorescent lights had flickered off sometime during our wait, and the fan had slowed to a stop; NEPA had taken away the light.

'The generator will come on soon,' the doctor said as he entered the room. In the dim light, he introduced himself. He was charming, tall and young, with a full head of hair. His loafers were black and shone even in the dim light. He was a rheumatologist, he said.

According to the X-ray, the doctor said, there were no fractures in the bone but there were patchy lucencies in the head of the clavicle and destructive changes in it.

Because of the destructive changes, he said, an abscess – a localized fluid collection – had formed in Mama's shoulder, a sign of infection in the area. He would insert a needle into the area where he was sure the abscess was located and drain it out. Then he would give Mama antibiotics through an IV to help ensure that the infection did not spread. She would have to be admitted to the hospital for all this to be done.

'You'll be just fine,' he said.

'It'll be fine,' I said to Mama, agreeing with the doctor. 'It'll be fine.'

I stayed at home with her the weeks after she was discharged, only leaving to run small errands: filling her prescription and stopping by the market to buy the ingredients for pepper soup.

My first day back at UniPort was about a month after Mama's discharge. I spent most of that day in a daze, not really hearing the lecturers, not taking notes in class. Outside of the lecture halls, I gazed at the other students, the wealthy ones who wore shiny shoes on their feet and, on their ears, tiny Bluetooth headsets – those wireless square buds, barely noticeable from a distance. I watched, transfixed by the way they displayed their wealth, the men swaggering, limping slightly on one leg, as if that leg were weak and dragged – in imitation of the way the American rap stars walked.

The girls had their own kind of swagger. They swayed their hips as they walked, hands dangling limply at their sides, as if they had no care in the world. Their patent leather handbags glistened, only a little less sparkly than the sequins on their stilettos. They drove Hondas and Jeeps. Their cell phones were always ringing, and they'd walk around saying 'darling' or 'sweetheart', their voices turning more and more saccharine as they spoke. Such good humour must have been from the soothing effect of having so much money, I thought, the effect of having so little to worry about. After all, there were only a few problems in life that money could not fix.

I was sitting on the cement steps of our classroom building when Njideka came to me.

'Na wetin dey trouble you?' she asked.

We were in the same government policy class. There were only two of us girls in the class. We would probably not have become friends if not for that. There could have been no two girls as different from each other. For one thing, her weave was always pristine. Sometimes I liked to imagine her head under all that artificial hair. I envisioned bald patches and a thinning hairline, and it was comforting to think that deep down, under all that perfection was a version of her that was just as imperfect as me.

That day, I shook my head and told her that nothing was the matter.

'Na your Mama?' she asked.

I did not answer.

She patted me on the shoulder, gently, then began to rub my back. She wore her weave in loose curls that day. They tumbled around her shoulders. A soft wind was blowing and carried in it the scent of her hair conditioner, something floral and welcoming, like the scent of bergamot.

And so, I told her. That Mama was in pain, and the doctors did not know the cause.

'You need good doctors,' Njideka said. 'Private doctors,

not those underpaid teaching-hospital doctors who are always going on strike.'

I shook my head bitterly and rolled my eyes at her. We could not even afford the teaching-hospital doctors. How would we afford the private doctors?

'At the private practices, they'll have state-of-the-art technology, not that old, broken-down equipment that you find in the teaching hospital. There'll be electricity, too,' Njideka said. 'Generators. No reliance on NEPA, which comes and goes like the wind.'

'Mama says it's the curse of the black bird,' I said. 'We'll just stick to praying for now.'

'Go to the private doctors,' Njideka said. A command. 'I know a good one I can refer you to.'

I shook my head. The sun was shining. The wind was stirring up the dust, and not too far from where we sat a light-coloured bird was perching on a branch. If this one would carry a mouse in its mouth and drop the mouse in front of our house, would it also be a curse? Or would its near-whiteness reverse the curse of the black bird?

'Do you hear me?' Njideka asked.

I nodded. And I told her honestly that we had no money. That, yes, Papa did have siblings, and although Mama did not have any siblings, she did have cousins. Yes, we even had some distant relatives, but they were all poor like us. Even if Mama or I had asked it of them, none of them would have had the financial means to help with Mama's visits to the specialists. Not that Mama's pride would ever allow her to ask it of them.

Njideka's phone began to vibrate then. She picked it up. 'Darling,' she said. Then she cupped the speaker of the phone and whispered to me, in proper English, words impressively articulated, the way I knew she would speak to whomever it was on the phone: 'I'll help you out,' she said. 'Stop by my place this afternoon. I'll be home.'

With that she was gone.

I went to her flat after my final class of the day. Mama would not worry. She expected that I'd be late, with having to catch up on so much missed schoolwork.

'I don't dash money,' Njideka said to me. 'It's not my style.'

I nodded. Not that I had come expecting that she would dash me the money for Mama's doctor visit. All the same, in case I ever felt the urge to ask, I now knew better.

Her voice was more vibrant than ever that afternoon. And I latched on to each and every one of her words, her intonations, because there was freedom in them, the way they rang out confidently, without restraint, without worry. Nothing like words between Mama and me.

Her primary patrons were the Yahoo Boys, she told me. They were the ones who rolled into town in sleek cars and with pockets full of cash, even American dollars. I had seen many fancy-looking young men around campus, but I had just assumed that they came from wealth. It had not crossed my mind until that visit with Njideka that many of them built their wealth on Internet fraud.

She also told me about the mugus, the older men, oil executives – often foreigners – overflowing with petro-naira. The mugus didn't hang around campus but in fancy restaurants and hotels. They bought her jewellery and paid for her recharge cards, sometimes paying as much as twenty thousand naira per month, because, of course, she had more than one phone.

'It's not hard work at all,' she said. 'Sometimes they just want you to have private dinners with them. Sometimes, they just want to look at and have an intelligent conversation with a pretty woman,' she said.

Her television was on, and from the corner of my eye I could see the images fluttering across the screen. The room was cool, because the air conditioner was also on. It was not something Mama or I had ever contemplated buying – an air conditioner, let alone a television that took up nearly half the surface of one wall. I had not even thought that such a television existed until I saw it in Njideka's flat.

'You could pay for your mama's bills with the money,' she said.

'Abeg, comot from here!' I said, glaring at her with my eyes wide open, shocked that she would even suggest such a thing for me. She could do as she pleased. But to go so far as to involve me in her sinful ways, that was another thing. 'Tufiakwa!' I said, snapping my fingers. 'God forbid!'

'You're a pretty girl,' Njideka said. 'Or at least you can be. And I know of a man who would love a girl like you.'

She tugged the scarf that I was wearing around my head. Thin braids fell loose around my shoulders. She stood up and disappeared into one of the rooms of the flat. She came back holding a wide mirror, and a bag of beauty products: nail polish, lipstick, eye pencil, lip liner, small boxes of blush and eyeshadow. 'Ten minutes,' she said, 'and I'll show you what you can look like.'

She brushed the hair at the base of my scalp, straightening out the tight curls. She rubbed powder on my face, smoothing it on with soft cotton balls. The movement of her fingertips was hypnotic. Slowly I surrendered myself to her hands. She rubbed blusher onto my cheeks. She finished with my lips. It was my same pale skin, my same bushy brows. But certain features had become magnified, and others had been changed, moulded to arrive at something more striking.

She took out a handful of plastic-wrapped packets from a small box that she had brought from the room. She stuck them in my purse. 'Condoms,' she said. 'Just in case.'

'I didn't say I'd do it,' I said.

'Your mama is sick, and there's a good chance you won't even have to sleep with the man.'

'My mama is waiting for me at home,' I said, tossing the condoms from my purse. I picked up my headscarf, along with my purse. 'It's sinful,' I said, and walked out the door.

Back at home, there was no light again, and I used a kerosene lantern to prepare Mama's pepper soup. She'd still not grown tired of the soup, or perhaps she was still clinging to the hope that it alone could cure her of the curse.

I'd grown tired of it. I roasted a plantain and ate that with some tomato stew.

That night, Mama asked me to help her bathe. For a week, she had only been able to give herself sponge baths, because it was too painful for her to climb in and out of the bath.

I boiled a kettle of water on the kitchen stove. We waited till the sun had gone down completely, then I poured the hot water into a bucket, took it to the tap outside and filled it with cool water so that the temperature was just right.

There was a cement slab in the backyard on which we washed our clothes. Above the slab were wire lines on which we hung the clothes to dry. Mama stood on the cement slab. She crouched a bit, as if shielding herself from peering eyes. But our fence ran the whole way around the compound, and the houses nearby were flats like ours, not high enough to allow the possibility of second-storey peeping Toms. Still she crouched, because of the pain. And though it was mostly dark outside, the moon and stars shined brightly enough that I could make out the redness all around her shoulder and chest.

With a small bowl, I poured the water over her shoulders, down her back. I lathered up a washcloth with a bar of soap and rubbed her skin gently with the cloth.

I poured the water down her breasts, lifted them one at a time and washed underneath. They were heavy and sagged, nothing like mine, though I knew that mine would surely one day become weighed down with age, too.

She squeezed her eyes shut each time the cloth touched her skin. It didn't matter how gentle I was. The fear had been implanted in her, and so she'd squeeze so hard that wrinkles formed on her forehead and crow's feet around her eyes. That night, it was hard to tell what the droplets on her face were: tears from so much pain and suffering, or merely splashes of bath water.

Even with the aroma of the soap, there was still something yeasty, almost stale, and a little honey-like about her scent. It was a smell that resembled that of the sweet powdered milk which we used to drink in our morning tea. And I thought, so this is what it smells like to be old and weak.

I imagined rubbing powder on her face, all over her body, smoothing her out, the way Njideka had smoothed me out. I imagined erasing the age from her face, imagined putting life into her cheeks. If only it could be as easy as rubbing some of Njideka's blush onto them. But of course, that was not an option.

We prayed again that night and Mama read again from Job. *Despise not thou the chastening of the Almighty: For He maketh sore, and bindeth up: He woundeth, and His hands make whole.*

★

'You must speak good English,' Njideka told me the next time we met. It was a Friday, after classes. I had told Mama that I would have to run some errands, university business, pick up groceries at the market. Those types of things. She had nodded and told me she'd be waiting, whenever it was that I got back home.

'None of this pidgin that we use when we are by ourselves,' Njideka said. 'These men are looking for intelligent women who can hold a conversation.' Of course, I could do just that. I could discuss budget and political issues comfortably. It was what I studied at the university. If I did well, I could bring in five hundred dollars or more. American dollars.

I would do it just that one night. To get the money for Mama. To get the money so that I could take her to a specialist, one that Njideka would recommend. I knew that Mama would ask where the money had come from. I'd tell her that I'd taken up a short-term job. It would be the truth. She'd probably ask more questions. *What kind of job? How did you find it?* I'd figure out answers for those questions later, I thought.

Njideka did my make-up just as she had that first afternoon. Then she lent me a red wrap-around dress, a little too tight on her, she said, but just my size. It formed a V around my neck. I'd never before given any thought to my collarbone, but in the mirror that evening, I thought what a beautiful thing the collarbone was. And I thought how terrible that Mama's was so damaged.

The man arrived in a BMW – a Be My Wife, Njideka teased. He was tall and dark, his simple linen buba and sokoto crisply ironed. He reached out and took my hand, drawing it upwards and tipping his head just a bit as he placed a kiss on its back. He wore gold rings on three of his five fingers. They were not massive rings, but small diamonds circled each of them and sparkled so that the rings appeared much larger than they actually were.

It was supposed to be a simple dinner, at one of those swanky restaurants in GRA – Blue Elephant or G's Barracuda – those expensive hangout spots for the wealthy. And it seemed that this would be the case as we headed down Abacha Road, past the GRA Everyday Emporium, the grocery store with the escalators and fancy security guards. But then he continued to drive, taking some turns and winding up in a place that, in the dark, I did not recognize. He stopped the car there and asked me to untie my dress. I shook my head, smiling just a bit, like a mother gently scolding a misbehaving child.

'Come on,' he said, his voice soft and pleading. 'Don't be afraid of me, beautiful Ada.'

My name on his tongue sounded vile. Like an insult.

'What about dinner?' I asked, trying to sound calm. 'Let's eat first, and then we'll go from there.'

'Come on,' he said again, his voice more gravelly, more urgent. He lifted his buba, lifted it so high that I could see the drawstring of his sokoto and the dark coils of hair just above, on his belly.

I shook my head again. 'Dinner first,' I said, my voice trembling. Njideka had said that most of the men wanted nothing beyond dinner and maybe a kiss. How could I have been so unlucky as to wind up with this man? I began to cry, begging him to take me back home.

He patted me on the back, then opened his door and stepped out. He came around to my side, pulled me out of the car and into the back seat, all the while telling me not to worry, that he would not hurt me. Then all his weight was on me and he was pinning open my thighs with his. He paused only to grab a condom from his pocket, to tear open its plastic wrap, and to slip it onto himself. I screamed, but it was dark all around, empty space like in an open field. Who could have heard?

He dropped me off several blocks away from Njideka's flat. It was just as well, I thought at first. But as soon as I got out of the car, I decided that I could not bear to see her. It would be like staring my sin straight in the face. It would have been too difficult a thing to do.

And so I walked home, many kilometres on bare feet, holding the sequined heels that Njideka had lent me. I found the stash of bills in my purse as I walked. One thousand dollars. All that money, perhaps because he knew that I had never been with a man. Maybe Njideka had told him. It was more than enough to pay for Mama's visits to a specialist.

Mama was kneeling by the sofa, her arms and chest resting on its cushion, as if she'd been in the middle of praying. She was wearing her grey wrapper tied around her chest. She turned slowly, her eyes probing. She must have seen the streaks of mascara coming down my face, the blotched lipstick around my mouth, the dried bits of blood that had dripped down my thighs, a darker shade of red than the dress I was wearing. I went to her, kneeled before her. But she only shook her head. 'Mama, ndo,' I said. Sorry.

Her eyes appeared sunken, and her shoulders were slumped lower than ever before. She only shook her head, and then she slowly walked away.

Days went by, and then weeks. I did not return to school, instead I remained at home with Mama. Every day I made her pepper soup and brought it to her. But each time I went back for the bowl, the soup was just as I had left it, only cold. She did not speak to me.

Then one Saturday, nearly two months later, I brought her pepper soup again in a tray, and for the first time since my night as a runs girl, she looked at me, her eyes dull. 'It's been a long time since we went to church,' she said. 'Tomorrow we should go.'

'Yes, Mama,' I said, but I wondered how she could possibly make it through the bus ride.

That evening I came back to collect her bowl of soup, and again, it was cold and untouched. She was leaning on the sofa again, as if about to pray.

I left her where she was and went off to wash the plates, to sweep the floors, to bathe. When I returned to her, she was still leaning on the couch. I called out to her. 'Mama! Do you hear me? Mama!' She did not respond. And then suddenly I was turning her around, checking for breath. And there was none.

Papa's brothers and sisters came to the funeral. Some of Mama's cousins came, too, along with some distant relatives, many of whom I did not recognize. 'Ekwensu,' they all called it, when I explained to them how the pain began. The work of the devil.

Together, we buried her in the cemetery not too far from our flat, the same place where we buried Papa. I used the money from my night as a runs girl to pay the funeral expense.

Sometimes I go to the cemetery to visit Mama and Papa. On days when I'm overwhelmed by shame, I go in the evening or at night, as if the darkness will somehow mask the shame. I allow myself to remember the time before Papa died, and if I listen carefully, I sometimes hear Mama's laughter ringing out, somewhere far away from the cemetery.

And sometimes I think that if I were to be placed in a valley full of bones, I would create a new Eve, create her from a new set of bones. And I would lay sinews upon her dry bones, and flesh upon the sinews. And I would cause there to be a noise, a clicking noise, and everything would fall in place. And I would cause breath to enter in, and this new Eve would live.

And this new Eve would walk amongst the trees of the garden. And she would drink from the waters of the river of the garden. And again, she would eat the forbidden fruit. But she would not be cast away from the garden, because she would be given the opportunity, just once, to ask for forgiveness. And she would be forgiven.

America

We drive through bushes. We pass the villages that rim our side of the Bonny River. The roads are sandy and brown, with open gutters, and with wrappers and cans and bottles strewn about. Collapsing cement shacks stand alongside the roads, in messy rows, like cartons that have long begun to decompose. There are hardly any trees, and the shrubs are little more than stumps, thin and dusty, not verdant as they used to be.

A short distance from us, something comes out of the river, a small boy or girl, maybe six or seven years old. Hands flail in the air and another child joins – typical children's play. Except that it's too early in the morning for that. Except that their skin, and even the cloth around their waist, gleams an almost solid black, that oily blackness of crude.

The bus moves slowly, and for a bit, as we make our way out of Port Harcourt, I worry it'll break down. The last time I made this trip (about a year ago now), there was a problem with the engine. The bus only made it to the terminal in Warri, not quite halfway between Port Harcourt and Lagos. When we arrived at the terminal, the driver asked us to exit. He locked the door to the bus and went inside one of the offices in the terminal. He locked the office door too, leaving us outside to fend for ourselves. We had passed no inns or motels on the way. Just splatters of small shops, their zinc roofs shining in the sun. Lots of green and yellowing grass. Clusters of trees.

At the terminal, I found a nice patch of ground on which I slept, using my luggage as a pillow under my head. Some passengers did the same. Others, I assume, wandered about the terminal all through the night. The next morning another bus arrived. It took us from Warri to Lagos. I made it just in time for my interview. Lucky that I had left a day in advance. Not that leaving in advance made much difference in the end: as with the two previous interviews, my application was declined.

I sit on the bus again, slightly more hopeful about the engine and much more hopeful about the interview. I have not left a day early, but so long as the bus does not break down, I expect that this interview will be a success. This time I have a plan and, even if I hesitate to be as assured as Gloria is, there is a good chance that she is right, that very soon I will be on my way to her.

It was on a dry and hot day in November that Gloria and I met. The headmistress had arranged it all: I would be Gloria's escort. I would show her around the campus for the week.

That day, the headmistress stood by her desk, me at her side, waiting for this Gloria Oke. I was already one of the senior teachers at the time; I had been at the school for nearly ten years by then.

I'd expected that she'd come in like the big madam she was, 'big' as in well-to-do and well known, maybe with a fancy buba and iro in lace, with a headscarf and maybe even the ipele shawl. Even with the heat, the headmistress, and all the big madams who visited our campus, came dressed that way.

But Gloria entered, tall and lanky, a bit too thin to be identified as a 'big madam'. She wore a long ivory-coloured gown, no fancy headscarf, no ipele hanging from her shoulder. Her unpermed hair was held together in a bun at the nape of her neck. Pale skin stuck out in contrast to dark brown eyes and hair. Her lips were natural, not lipstick red. On her feet she wore a simple pair of black flats.

Even then, there were things I liked about her: the way her eyes seemed unsure, not being able to hold my gaze. The way she stuttered her name, as if unconvinced of her own existence in the world. And yet her voice was strong and firm, something of a paradox.

That first day, we spent our lunch break together, and for the rest of the week we did the same, me sharing my fried plantain with her, and she, her rice and stew with me.

She started to visit me at my flat after her week at the school was up. She'd stop by every other week or so, on the weekends when we could spend more than a few hours together. I'd make us dinner, jollof rice, beans and yams, maybe some garri and soup. We'd spend the evening chatting or just watching the news. Sometimes we'd walk around the neighbourhood and when we returned, she'd pack her things and leave.

I grew a big enough garden in my backyard. Pineapple leaves stuck out in spikes from the earth, neat rows of them. Plantain trees stood just behind the pineapple leaves. Behind the plantain trees, lining the wall leading up to the gate of the flat, an orange tree grew, and a guava tree, and a mango tree.

Once, while we stood plucking a ripe mango, Gloria asked me what it was like to teach science at the school. Did we conduct experiments or just study from a book? Were all of the students able to afford the books? It was a private school, she knew, but she suspected (quite accurately) that that didn't mean all the students were able to afford the texts.

I straightened up to face the wall that led up to the metal gate. Lizards were racing up and down. I told her that teaching was not my job of choice. That I'd rather be doing something more hands-on, working directly with the earth, like in my garden. Maybe something to do with the environment, with aquatic ecology: running water-quality reports, performing stream classification, restoration, wetland determinations, delineations, design and monitoring. But there were none of those jobs during the time I did my job search, even though there should have been plenty of them, especially with the way things were going for the Niger Delta.

But even if the jobs had been available, I said, perhaps they would have been too dangerous for me, with all that bunkering going on, criminal gangs tapping the oil straight from the pipelines and transporting it abroad to be sold illegally. The rebel militias stealing the oil, and refining it, and selling it to help pay for their weapons. All those explosions from old oil rigs that had been left abandoned by Shell. Perhaps it would have been too dangerous a thing.

She was standing with her hands on her hips, showing surprise only with her eyes. I suppose it was understandable that she would have assumed I loved my job to have stayed those many years.

We became something – an item, Papa says – in February, months after Gloria's visit to the school. That evening, I was hunched over, sweeping my apartment with a broom, the native kind, made from the raw and dry stems of palm leaves, tied together at the thick end with a bamboo string. I imagine it's the kind of broom that Gloria no longer sees, the kind that Americans have probably never seen.

Gloria must have come in through the back door of the flat (she often did), through the kitchen and into the parlour. I was about to collect the dirt into the dustpan when she entered.

She brought with her a cake, a small one with white icing

and spirals of silver and gold. On top of it was a white-striped candle, moulded in the shape of the number thirty-four. She set it on the coffee table in the parlour and carefully lit the wick.

I set the broom and dustpan down and straightened up. Gloria reached out to tuck strands of my tattered hair back into place. I'd barely blown out the flame when she dipped her finger into the cake's icing and took a taste of it. Then she dipped her finger into the icing again and held the clump out to me.

'Take,' she said, almost in a whisper, smiling her shyest sort of smile.

Just then, the phone began to ring: a soft, buzzing sound. We heard the ring but neither of us turned to answer, because even as it was ringing, I was kissing the icing off Gloria's finger. By the time the ringing was done, I was kissing it off her lips.

Mama still reminds me every once in a while that there are penalties in Nigeria for that sort of thing. And of course, she's right. I've read of them in the newspapers and have heard of them on the news. Still, sometimes I want to ask her to explain to me what she means by 'that sort of thing', as if it is something so terrible that it does not deserve a name, as if it is so unclean that it cannot be termed 'love'. But then I remember that evening and I cringe, because, of course, I know she can explain; she's seen it with her eyes.

That evening, the phone rings, and if I had answered, it would have been Mama on the line. But instead, I remain with Gloria, allowing her to trace her fingers across my brows, allowing her to trace my lips with her own. My heart thumps in my chest and I feel the thumping of her heart. She runs her fingers down my belly, lifting my blouse slightly, hardly a lift at all. And then her hand is travelling lower, and I feel myself tightening, and I feel the pounding all over me. Suddenly, Mama is calling my name, calling it loudly, so that I have to look up to see if I'm not just hearing things. We have made our way to the sofa and, from there, I see Mama shaking her head, telling me that the wind has blown and the bottom of the fowl has been exposed.

Mama stands where she is for just a moment longer; all the while she is staring at me with a sombre look in her eyes. 'So, this is why you won't take a husband?' she asks. It is an interesting thought, but not one I'd ever really considered. Left to myself, I would have said that I'd just not found the right man. But it's not that I'd ever been particularly interested in dating men anyway.

'A woman and a woman cannot bear children,' Mama says to me. 'That's not the way it works.' As she stomps out of the room, she says again, 'The wind has blown and the bottom of the fowl has been exposed.'

I lean my head on the glass window of the bus and I try to imagine how the interview will go. But every so often the bus hits a bump and jolts me out of my thoughts.

There is a woman sitting to the right of me. Her scent is strong, somewhat like the scent of fish. She wears a head scarf, which she uses to wipe the beads of sweat that form on her face. Mama used to sweat like this. Sometimes she'd call me to bring her a cup of ice. She'd chew on the blocks of ice, one after the other, and then request another cup. It was the real curse of womanhood, she said. The heart palpitations, the dizzy spells, the sweating that came with the cessation of the flow. That was the real curse. Cramps were nothing in comparison, she said.

The woman next to me wipes her sweat again. I catch a

strong whiff of her putrid scent. She leans her head on the seat in front of her, and I ask her if everything is fine.

'The baby,' she says, lifting her head back up. She rubs her belly and mutters something under her breath.

'Congratulations,' I say. And after a few seconds I add, 'I'm sorry you're not feeling well.'

She tells me that it comes with the territory. That it's been two years since she and her husband married, and he was starting to think that there was some defect in her. 'So, actually,' she tells me, 'this is all cause for celebration.'

She turns to the seat on her right where there are two black-and-white-striped polythene bags. She pats one of the bags and there is that strong putrid scent again. 'Stock fish,' she says, 'and dried egusi and ogbono for soup.' She tells me that she's heading to Lagos, because that is where her in-laws live. There will be a ceremony for her there, and she is on her way to help with the preparations. Her husband is taking care of business in Port Harcourt, but he will be heading down soon, too, to join in celebrating the conception of their first child.

'Boy or girl?' I ask, feeling genuinely excited for her.

'We don't know yet,' she says. 'But either one will be a real blessing for my marriage. My husband has never been happier,' she says.

I turn my head to look out the window, but then I feel her gaze on me. When I look back at her, she asks if I have a husband or children of my own.

I think of Mama and I think of Gloria. 'No husband, no children,' I say.

The day I confessed to him about Gloria, Papa said: 'When a goat and yam are kept together, either the goat takes a bite of the yam, bit by bit, or salivates for it. That is why when two adults are always seen together, it is no surprise when the seed is planted.'

I laughed and reminded him that there could be no seed planted with Gloria and me.

'No,' he said, reclining on his chair, holding the newspaper that he was never reading, just always intending to read. 'No, there can be no seed,' he said.

It had been Mama's idea that I tell him. He would talk some sense into me, she said. All this Gloria business was nonsense. Woman was made for man. Besides, what good was it living a life in which you had to go around afraid of getting caught? Mobile policemen were always looking for that sort of thing – men with men or women with women. And the penalties were harsh. Jail time, fines, stoning or flogging, depending on where in Nigeria you were caught. And you could be sure that it would make the news. Public humiliation. What kind of life was I expecting to have, always having to turn around to check if anyone was watching? 'Your Papa must know of it,' she said. 'He will talk some sense into you. You must tell him of it. If you don't, I will.'

But Papa took it better than Mama had hoped. Like her, he warned me of the dangers. But 'love is love', he said.

Mama began to cry then. 'Look at this skin,' she said, stretching out her hands to me. She grabbed my hand and placed it on her arm. 'Feel it,' she said. 'Do you know what it means?' she asked, but did not wait for my response. 'I'm growing old,' she said. 'Won't you stop being stubborn and take a husband, give up that silly thing with that Gloria friend of yours, bear me a grandchild before I'm dead and gone?'

'People have a way of allowing themselves to get lost in America,' Mama said when I told her that Gloria would be going. Did I remember Chinedu Okonkwo's daughter who went abroad to study medicine and never came back? I nodded. I did remember. And Obiageli Ojukwu's sister who married that button-nosed American and left with him so many years ago? Did I remember that she promised to come back home to raise her children? Now the children were grown, and still no sight of them. 'But it's a good thing in this case,' Mama said smugly. She was sitting on a stool in the veranda, fanning herself with a plantain leaf. Gloria and I had been together for two years by then, the two years since Mama walked in on us. In that time, Gloria had written many more articles on education policies, audacious criticisms of our government, suggesting more effective methods of standardizing the system, suggesting that those in control of government affairs needed to better educate themselves. More and more of her articles were being published in local and national newspapers, the *Tribune*, *Punch*, the *National Mirror* and such.

Universities all over the country began to invite her to give lectures on public policies and education strategy. Soon she was getting invited to conferences and lectures abroad. And before long, she was offered that post in America, in that place where water formed a cold, feather-like substance called snow, which fell leisurely from the sky in winter. Pretty, like white lace.

'I thought her goal was to make Nigeria better, to improve Nigeria's education system,' Papa said.

'Of course,' Mama replied. 'But, like I said, America has a way of stealing all our good ones from us. When America calls, they go. And more times than not, they stay.'

Papa shook his head. I rolled my eyes.

'Perhaps she's only leaving to escape scandal,' Mama said.

'What scandal?' I asked.

'You know. That thing between you two.'

'That thing is private, Mama,' I said. 'It is between us two, as you say. And we work hard to keep it that way.'

'What do her parents say?' Mama asked.

'Nothing.' It was true. She'd have been a fool to let them know. They were quite unlike Mama and Papa. They went to church four days out of the week. They lived the words of the Bible as literally as they could. Not like Mama and Papa, who were that rare sort of Nigerian Christian who had a faint, shadowy sort of respect for the Bible, the kind of faith that required no works.

'With a man and a woman, there'd be no need for so much privacy,' Mama said that day. 'Anyway, it all works out for the best.' She paused to wipe with her palms the sweat that was forming on her forehead. 'I'm not getting any younger,' she continued. 'And I even have the names picked out!'

'What names?' I asked.

'For a boy, Arinze. For a girl, Nkechi. Pretty names.'

'Mama!' I said, shaking my head at her.

'Perhaps now you'll be more inclined to take a husband,' she said. 'Why waste such lovely names?'

The first year she was gone, we spoke on the phone at least once a week, but the line was filled with static and there were empty spots in the reception, blank spaces into which our voices faded. I felt the distance then.

Still Gloria continued to call, and we took turns re-constructing the dropped bits of conversation, stubbornly rein-serting them into the line, stubbornly resisting the emptiness.

The end of that first year, she came back for a visit. She was still the same Gloria, but her skin had turned paler and she had put on a bit of weight.

'You're turning white,' I teased.

'It's the magic of America,' she teased back. And then she laughed. 'It's no magic at all,' she said. 'Just lack of sunlight. Lots of sitting at the desk, writing, and planning.'

Perhaps she was right. But it was the general consensus in Port Harcourt (and I imagine in most of Nigeria) that things were better in America. I was convinced of it. I heard it in the way her voice was even softer than before. I saw it in the relaxed looks on the faces of the people in the pictures she brought. Pictures of beautiful landscapes, clean places, not littered at all with cans and wrappers like our roads. Snow, white and soft, like clouds having somehow descended on land. Pictures of huge department stores in which everything seemed to sparkle. Pictures in which cars and buildings shone, where even the skin of fruit glistened.

By the time her visit was over, we had decided that I would try to join her in America, that I would see about getting a visa. If not to be able to work there, then at least to study and earn an American degree. Because, though she intended eventually to come back to Nigeria, there was no telling how long she would end up staying in America. The best thing for now was that I try to join her there.

I think of Gloria as my head jerks back and forth against the window of the bus. I try to imagine her standing in a landscape like the one in the pictures she's sent. A lone woman surrounded by tall cedars and oaks. Even if it's only June, the ground in my imagination is covered with white snow, looking like a bed of bleached cotton balls. This is my favourite way to picture her in America.

I think back to my first interview. The way the man dismissed me even before I could answer why I wanted so badly to attain a visa for the USA. The second interview was not much different. That time, I was able to respond. And then the man told me how foolish I was for expecting that a job would be waiting for me in America. I held an African degree; was I unaware of this? How could I even hope to compete with all the other job applicants who would probably not be from an African country, whose degrees would certainly be valued more than any Nigerian degree ever would?

I cried the entire bus ride back to Port Harcourt after that second interview. When I got home, I told Mama and Papa what I had done. It was the first time they were hearing about my plan to join Gloria in America. By this time, she had been gone over two years.

Papa was encouraging. He said not to give up. If it was an American degree I needed, then go ahead and apply to American schools so that I could have that American degree. It would be good for me to be in America, he said, a place where he imagined I could be free with the sort of love that I had for Gloria.

'It's not enough that I won't have a grandchild in all of this,' Mama said, after hearing what Papa had to say. 'Now I must deal with losing my only child, too.' There were tears in her eyes. And then she asked me to promise that I would not allow myself to get lost in America.

I shook my head and promised her that she'd not be losing me at all.

All the while, the woman I loved was there, worlds away. If I didn't make it that third time, I thought, there was a good chance she'd grow weary of waiting for me. If I were to be once more declined, she might move on and start loving somebody else.

★

By the time I booked the third appointment I had already gained admission to one of the small colleges near where Gloria lived in America. All that remained was for me to be approved for the visa.

About a month before the third interview, Gloria called me to tell me the news. An oil rig had exploded. Thousands of barrels of crude were leaking out into the Gulf per day. Perhaps even hundreds of thousands, there was no telling for sure. She was watching it on the television. Arresting camera shots of something like black clouds forming in waters that would usually be clear and blue.

It was evening when she called, and mosquitoes were whistling about the parlour of my flat. They were landing on the curtains and on the tables and on the walls, making tiny shadows wherever they perched. And I thought how there were probably no mosquitoes where she was. Did mosquitoes even exist in America?

'A terrible spill in the Gulf,' she told me. 'Can you imagine?' she asked.

I told her that I could not. It was the truth. America was nothing like Nigeria, after all. Here, roads were strewn with trash and it was rare that anyone cared to clean them up. Here, spills were expected. Because we were just Africans. What did Shell care? Here, the spills were happening on a weekly basis. But a spill like that in America? I could honestly not imagine.

'It's unfortunate,' I said to Gloria.

'Something good must be made out of such an unfortunate event,' she said.

The bus picks up speed. I watch through the windows as we pass by the small villages in Warri. Then we are driving by signs for Sapele and for the Ologbo Game Reserve. The bus is quiet, and the woman next to me is fast asleep, and I wonder how she can stand to sleep on such a bumpy ride. Hours later, we pass the signs for the Lekki Lagoon. We reach Lagos at about 2 p.m., an early arrival for which I'm very thankful, because it gives me plenty of time to make my way to the embassy on Victoria Island.

At 3 p.m., I arrive at Walter Carrington Crescent, the road on which the embassy is located. Inside the building, I wait in a small room with buzzing fluorescent lights. There is an oscillating floor fan in the corner, and a window is open, but the air is still muggy and stale. I think of Gloria and I imagine what she is doing. It is morning where she is in America, and perhaps she's already at her office at the university, jotting down notes at her desk, preparing lectures for her students, or perhaps even rehearsing for a public reading somewhere.

I imagine her in a gown, something simple and unpretentious, with her hair plaited in braids, the way it used to be. It's gathered into a bun at the nape of her neck, but there are loose strands dangling down her back. Just the way she was the first time I saw her.

I continue to wait. The fan oscillates, and I trace its rotations with my eyes. I think of the spill and I remember Gloria's description: *something like black clouds forming in waters that would usually be clear and blue.* The waters of the Niger Delta were once clear and blue. Now the children wade in the water and come out with Shell oil glowing on their skin.

I'm imagining stagnant waters painted black and brown with crude when finally someone calls my name. The voice is harsh and causes me to think of gravel, of rock-strewn roads, the kinds filled with potholes the size of washbasins, the kind of potholes we see all over Nigeria, the kind I imagine America does not have.

I answer the call with a smile plastered on my face. But all the while my heart is palpitating – rapid, irregular beats that only I can hear. They are loud and distracting, like raindrops on zinc.

The man who calls my name is old and grey-haired and wears suspenders over a yellow-white short-sleeved shirt. He doesn't smile at me, just turns quickly around and leads me down a narrow corridor. He stops at the door of a small room and makes a gesture with his hand, motioning me to enter. He does not follow me into the room, which is more an enclosed cubicle than a room; instead there is a clicking sound behind me. I turn around to see that the door has been shut.

In the room, another man sits on a swivel chair, the kind with thick padding, and expensive grey-and-white cloth covering. He stands up as I walk towards him. His skin is tan, but a pale sort of tan. He says hello, and his words come out a little more smoothly than I am accustomed to, levelled and under-accentuated, as if his tongue has somehow flattened the words, as if it has somehow diluted them in his mouth. An American.

He wears a black suit with pin stripes, a dress shirt with the two top buttons undone, no tie; and he looks quite seriously at me. He reaches across the table, which is more like a counter, to shake my hand. He wears three rings, each on its own finger, excepting the index and the thumb. The stones in the rings sparkle as they reflect the light.

He offers me the metal stool across from him. When I am seated, he asks for my papers: identification documents; invitation letter; bank records.

'Miss Nnenna Etoniru,' he begins, pronouncing my name in his diluted sort of way. 'Tell me your occupation.'

'Teacher,' I say.

'Place of employment,' he says, not quite a question.

'Federal Government Girls' College in Abuloma. I work there as a science teacher.'

'A decent job.'

I nod. 'Yes, it's a good enough job,' I say.

He lifts up my letter of invitation. The paper is thin and from the back I can see the swirls of Gloria's signature. 'Who is this Miss Gloria Oke?' he asks. 'Who is she to you?'

'A friend,' I say. And that answer is true.

'A friend?'

'A former co-worker, too.' I tell him that we met years ago at the Federal Government Girls' College in Abuloma. That we became friends when she was invited to help create a new curriculum. He can check the school records if he wishes, I say, confidently of course, because that answer, too, is true.

Next question: proof of funding. I direct him to the bank statements, not surprisingly, from Gloria. He mumbles under his breath. Then he looks up at me and mutters something about how lucky I am to have a friend like her. Not many people he knows are willing to fund their friends' education abroad, he says.

Then the big question. Why not just study here in Nigeria? There are plenty of Nigerian universities that offer a Master's in Environmental Engineering, he says. Why go all the way abroad to study what Nigerian universities offer here at home?

The question doesn't shock me, because I've anticipated and rehearsed it many more times than I can count in the month since that phone conversation with Gloria.

I begin by telling him of the oil spill in America. He seems to be unaware of it. I tell him that it has drawn some attention for Nigeria, for our plight with the Niger Delta. I tell him that going to America will allow me to learn first-hand the measures that the US government is taking in their attempt to deal with the aftermath of their spill. Because it's about time we Nigerians found ways to handle our own.

He doesn't question me about how I expect to connect with the US government. He doesn't ask how exactly I expect to learn first-hand about their methods of dealing with that type of environmental disaster. Perhaps, having made a life for himself here in Nigeria, he, too, has begun to adopt the Nigerian mentality. Perhaps he, too, has begun to see the US the way most of us Nigerians do: as an abstraction, a sort of Utopia, a place where you go for answers, a place that always has those answers waiting for you.

I tell him about the area around the Bonny River. I tell him that the vegetation there once thrived. That the trees grew tall, and from them sprang green leaves. And their flowers gave rise to fruit. Of course, that memory is not mine, I say. It is my mother's. From a former reality, one too old to be my own.

I tell him that decades ago, before the pipes began to burst (or maybe even before Shell came into the area – and of course, these days it's hard to remember a time without Shell), Gio Creek was filled with tall, green mangroves. Birds flew and sang in the skies above the creek, and there was plenty of fish and crab and shrimp in the waters below. Now the mangroves are dead, and the birds are gone. There are no fish, no shrimp, and no crab to be caught. Instead, oil shoots up in the air, like a fountain of black water; and fishermen lament that rather than coming out of the water with fish, they are instead harvesting Shell oil on their bodies.

I tell him that areas like these have undergone what amounts to the American spill, only every year for fifty years. Oil pouring out every week, killing our land, our ecosystem. A resource that should make us rich, instead causing our people to suffer. 'It's the politics,' I say. 'But I'm no politician.' Instead, I tell him, I'd like to see if we can't at least construct efficient and effective mechanisms for cleaning up the damage that has been done. I tell him that Nigeria will benefit from sending out students to study and learn from the recent spill in the US, to learn methods of dealing with such a recurrent issue in our own Niger Delta.

He nods enthusiastically at me. He says what a shame it is that the Nigerian government can't get rid of all the corruption. He tells me that the government officials themselves are corrupt. 'Giving foreigners power over their own oil, pocketing for themselves the money that these foreigners pay for the oil.'

I look at him, in his fancy suit and rings. I wonder if he is not himself pocketing some of that oil money. But something good must be made out of such an unfortunate event. And so, I don't question the man in the suit about where the money for his rings or suit is coming from.

He fusses with the collar of his shirt and says, 'Sometimes when Nigerians go to America, they get their education and begin to think they are too cultured and sophisticated to come back home.' He pauses. Then, 'How do we know that you will?'

I think of Mama. 'I don't intend to get lost in America,' I say, more confidently than I feel. Because even as I say it, there is a part of me that is afraid that I will want to get lost in America. There is a part of me hoping that I will find that new life much less complicated, much more trouble-free than the one here. Still, I say it confidently, because saying it so might help me to keep Mama's fear from becoming a reality. Because I know that it might break Mama's heart if I were to break my promise to her. But mostly, I say it confidently because Gloria is on my mind, and if I am to be granted permission to go and be with her, then I must give the man the answer I know he wants: an emphatic vow that I will come back home.

He smiles and congratulates me as he hands me the green-coloured card. He takes my passport from me and tells me to come back in two days.

The sun is setting as I make my way down Walter Carrington Crescent. I look up. There are orange and purple streaks in the sky, but instead of thinking of those streaks, I find myself thinking of white snow, shiny metals reflecting the light of the sun. And I think of Gloria playing in the snow – like I imagine Americans do – lying in it, forming snow angels on the ground. I think of Papa suggesting that perhaps America would be the best place for me and my kind of love. I think of my work at the Federal Government Girls' College. In America, after I have finished my studies, I'll finally be able to find the kind of job I want. I think how I can't wait to get on the plane.

I cross over to the next street. It is narrow, but there are big houses on each side of it, the kinds with metal gates, and fancy gatemen with uniforms and berets, and small sheds like mini-houses near the gates, sheds in which the gatemen stay.

I imagine the insides of the houses: leather couches and stainless-steel appliances imported from America; flat-screen televisions hanging even in the bathrooms, American-style.

But the road just in front of these houses, just outside the nice gates, is filled with potholes, large ones. And in the spaces between the houses, that corridor that forms where one gate ends and the next begins, there are piles of car tyres, planks of deteriorating wood, layered one on top of another. Shattered glass, empty barrels of oil, sweet wrappers, food wrappers, old batteries, crumpled paper, empty soda cans.

I stop at the entrance of one of these corridors. Two

chickens squirm about, zigzagging through the filth, jutting their necks back and forth, sniffing and pecking at the garbage, diffident pecks, as if afraid of poison.

I tell myself to continue walking, to ignore all of this foulness, just like the owners of the big houses have managed to do. Maybe it's even their garbage that saturates these alleyways, as if the houses themselves are all that matter, and the roads leading to them inconsequential.

But for me, it is a reluctant kind of disregard that stems from a feeling of shame: shame that all that trash should even exist there, shame that empty barrels should be there, between the fancy houses, littering the roads after the oil they once contained has been made to do its own share of littering.

Several streets down, I find a hotel, not one of the fancy ones, more just an inn. The room to which I am assigned smells musty and stale, and I can feel the dust on my skin.

I scratch my arms with the edges of the green-coloured card. I think of the possibilities, of the many ways in which I might profit from the card. I am still scratching and making plans for America when I drift into sleep.

The story should end there, but it doesn't. A person wishes for something so long that when it finally happens, she should be nothing but grateful. What sympathy can we have for someone who, after wanting something so badly for three long years, realizes almost as soon as she's gotten it that perhaps she's been wrong in wanting it all that time?

My second night at the inn, the night before I am to return to the embassy for my paperwork and passport, I think of Mama, her desire for a grandchild, and I think: Isn't it only natural that she'd want a grandchild? I think of the small children emerging from the waters of the Delta covered in black crude. Their playground destroyed by the oil war. And I think: Who's to say that this won't some day be the case even in America? It all starts small by small. And then it gets out of hand. And here I am running away from one disaster only find myself in a place that might soon also begin to fall apart.

There is a folk tale that Mama used to tell me when I was still in primary school. She'd tell it in the evenings when there was not much else to do, those evenings when NEPA had taken light away and there was no telling when they'd return it. I'd sit on a bamboo mat, and she'd light a candle, allow its wax to drip onto the bottom of an empty can of evaporated milk, a naked can, without its paper coating. She'd stick the candle on the wax and allow it to harden in place. And then she'd begin the story.

In the dim candlelight, I'd observe the changes that took place on her face with each turn of her thought. Soft smiles turned to wrinkles in the forehead, then to distant, disturbed eyes which then refocused, becoming clear again like a smoggy glass window whose condensation had been dispelled suddenly by a waft of air.

The folk tale was about an imprudent little boy, Nnamdi, whose wealthy father had been killed by a wicked old man who envied his wealth. Having killed Nnamdi's father, the wicked old man steals all of the family's possessions so that Nnamdi and his mother are left with not even a small piece of land on which they can live. And so it is that they make their new home in the bush. There they find a two-month-old goat kid, a stray, with a rope around its neck. Nnamdi's mother ties the goat to a tall iroko tree. Still, they continue to eat the green and purple leaves of the plants in the bush for food, because Nnamdi's mother decides that they are to save the goat. It will grow, she says, and when it does she will sell it for so much money that they will be able to move out of the bush, or at least to build a nice house for themselves there.

But one day, foolish Nnamdi leads the goat by its rope into the market place, and he sells it to a merchant who gives him a bagful of what the boy assumes is money. But when he returns to the bush, to his mother, Nnamdi opens the bag to find several handfuls of udara seeds, some still soggy, coated thinly with the flesh of the fruit.

His mother, angry at him not only for selling the goat, but also for doing so in exchange for mere seeds, furiously tosses them into the bush. The next morning, Nnamdi finds that a tall udara tree has grown, taller even than the iroko, so tall that its tips reach into the soft white clouds in the sky.

Nnamdi climbs the tree against his mother's wishes. In the uppermost branches, he finds a large, stately house-in-the-sky. He parts the branches, those thin stalks at the tip of the tree, and pushes through the rustling leaves. He arrives at an open window and enters the house that way. First he calls out to see if anyone is home. Once. Twice. There is no response.

There is a large table not far from the window. Nnamdi walks to the table. It is covered with a white cloth fringed with silk tassels. Nnamdi runs his fingers across the tassels. In the air, there is the scent of something savoury, a little curried, perhaps even a little sweet. Nnamdi follows the scent into the kitchen and there, on the stove, the lid of a large pot rattles as steam escapes from beneath. Nnamdi lifts the lid and breathes in the savoury scent. And then he sees it, through the doorway of the kitchen, in the parlour: a lustrous cage sitting atop a white cushion. The cushion is nearly as tall as he is. Inside the cage is a golden hen, perched on the top half of the hutch. All over the parlour floor, he sees coins, glistening like the cage. Glistening like the hen.

Nnamdi goes into the parlour. He climbs the cushion and takes the hen. By one wall of the parlour, lined on the floor, are half a dozen small bags. Nnamdi peeks into them and sees that they are filled with more gold coins. He ties some of the bags around his waist, others he fastens to the hem of his shorts. He removes his shirt and makes a sack out of it. He slings the sack across his chest and carefully places the golden hen inside.

The wicked old man returns in time to see Nnamdi climbing down the udara tree. He pursues the boy, catching him just as Nnamdi leaps from one branch to the next, catching him by the bag of coins that is fastened to his shorts. But Nnamdi manages to escape the old man's grasp. He wriggles away, leaving the old man with just the bag of coins.

Nnamdi takes off once more, gains ground, and finally lands safely in the bush. In fact, he gains so much ground that he is able to begin chopping down the udara tree before his pursuer has made it past the halfway point. Feeling the sudden swaying of the tree, the wicked old man scrambles back up to his home in the clouds before the tree falls. But he scrambles back without his golden hen, and with only that one bag of coins.

The story always stopped there, and then I'd pester Mama to tell me more. 'What about the rest?' I'd ask. Did the hen continue to produce the gold coins? If so, for how much longer? And what did Nnamdi and his mother do with the coins? Did they build for themselves a huge mansion right there in the bush? Or did Nnamdi give all the coins away like he did with the goat? Did he perhaps even give the hen itself away? Did they all live happily ever after?

'There's no rest,' Mama would say. Or sometimes, 'The rest is up to you.'

That night, my final night in the inn, I sit on my bed and I recall every twist of that folk tale. I think of crude. And I think of gold. And I think of crude as gold. I imagine Nigeria – the land and its people – as the hens, the producers of the gold. And I think that even when all the gold is gone, there will always be the hens to produce more gold. But what happens when all the hens are gone, when they have either run away or have been destroyed? Then what?

The next day, I collect my paperwork from the embassy, and hours later, I head back to Port Harcourt to pack my bags. The bus bounces along the potholed roads, causing my head and heart to jolt this way and that. But I force my eyes shut as if shutting them tight will prevent me from changing my mind, as if shutting them tight will keep regret from making its way to me.

Shelter

It wasn't that Mama never tried to take us away. There was that once she did. We were on Buswell Street then. I was in middle school, merely eleven or twelve years old.

We used to watch that old television, the one with the broken antenna, which stuck up weakly like the tentacles of an injured animal. That day *E.T.* was showing on the screen, his eyes big and blue. Wrinkled E.T., looking like an overgrown lizard.

I was gawking at the screen when I heard the jingling of Papa's keys. The door flung open. He entered, went straight to their room. Suddenly his voice was booming, and Mama's little voice was countering; but it was hardly a counter at all.

When she finally came out of the room, there was blood dribbling down one side of her lips. Papa followed her, shouting and flailing his hands. I watched them both from where I sat, afraid to go between them and all his anger.

She went into the kitchen. He followed her. I stood up from where I sat and followed them both. I stopped at the entrance of the kitchen, that doorway without a door, just like the doorway leading from the parlour into the kitchen of our old Port Harcourt house. I continued to watch.

At the sink, he hovered above her, muttering now, no longer shouting. Perhaps speaking that way was the best he could do to gain back control of his anger. He spoke that way as she turned on the tap, and as she bent her head towards the running water. He was still speaking that way as she washed the blood off her face. But then he lost control once more, and the muttering turned back to shouting.

She straightened up and made to walk away, but he closed the space between them, grabbed her by the shoulders, then by the hair, pushed and pushed so that eventually she was down on her knees. I rushed into the kitchen then, wriggling my little body between them, screaming and screaming for him to let go. Eventually he did.

That evening, Mama took me to the ice-cream shop in Brookline. One vanilla ice-cream cone for me. None for her. She held my hand and we walked together to the park. It was early summer, evening, but the sun was shining. The ice cream dripped down the sides of my cone.

We took turns teeter-tottering on the see-saw. We did not speak. She kept her eyes at a vanishing point behind me, far beyond where I sat on the see-saw, far beyond the trees, perhaps even as far as the horizon, where the sun hung like an orange ball in the sky. I observed her swollen lips, the side where Papa's fist must have landed. Only when the sun began to set did she step off the see-saw. She came around to my side and held out her hand to me.

We had just turned the corner onto Buswell Street when we saw the woman. If it had been Sunday morning, before 9 a.m., she would have been inside the church, handing out cans of beans, boxes of Fruit Loops, loaves of bread.

But it was a weekday, not a day for the food bank. Perhaps she had just come out of one of those evening weekday masses, or perhaps she had just finished some other work at the church, because there she stood, a few steps in front of the church, waiting for the bus, the street lamp hanging above her, shining brightly over her head.

It was she who first waved to Mama, and of course, Mama waved back. And then she was signalling us with her hands to come over to her, and we did.

At first there was that smile on her face, but then her face turned serious, her mouth tightening into a circle. She stared at Mama's lips, stared at mine as if expecting to find something similar to Mama's. Her eyes were blue, and for a moment I thought of E.T. That deep blueness of his eyes.

'What happened?' she asked, her eyes narrowing with concern.

There were faint evening sounds – car engines passing by, birds and crickets singing in the dark. And suddenly Mama was crying, that serious kind of cry: her shoulders heaved, her breath caught. I leaned into her, held her hand even tighter than before.

Words came out of both of their mouths, Mama's words hurried and inquiring and thick with her accent, the woman's soothing and kind and flowing, the smooth way in which I had come to expect American speech to flow.

I thought of Papa in the apartment, wondered what would happen if he were suddenly to walk by and find Mama crying, if he were suddenly to walk by and find Mama telling the woman about the things he did to us. Surely he would lead her straight home and would let her have it again. Or maybe even, if he were furious enough, he would let her have it right there, in front of the woman. Not that he had ever done a thing like that in public before.

Still, a person did not go around with black eyes and swollen lips and such without people suspecting. The woman had surely seen it before – a black eye on Mama, or a purple-black bruise on my arm – as we stood in line collecting food from her.

Even at school, Mrs Stephens used to ask about the bruises. I'd tell her how I had fallen off the swing, or how I had accidentally caught my arms in the rope of the swing. Always the swing.

Mrs Stephens would nod at me suspiciously, and eventually I began to wear only long-sleeved shirts, and trousers, even when the weather became hot and muggy, even when the humidity made the fabric of my clothes cling to my skin.

We stood there. After a while, the woman looked into her handbag, pulled out a small card, wrote a number on it.

Mama wiped away her tears, accepted the card, nodded.

Soon the bus screeched to a stop, and the woman climbed inside.

We walked the rest of the way home, Mama and I, neither of us saying a word. Not a word as she quietly unlocked the door. Not a word as she quietly turned the knob. She knew Papa would be asleep by then. She did not want to wake him up.

She did not call. Not the next day. Not the day after. Weeks went by. A month. Two months. Each day that passed, I thought of the card, imagined it sinking lower and lower in Mama's purse, imagined it arriving at the very bottom, disappearing there, among all her other outdated or unused notes – grocery lists and reminders – dog-eared, wrinkled and forgotten. Lurking in that abyss. Waiting to be gathered and thrown away.

Eventually, I stopped imagining the card.

Then one evening, we went again to the ice-cream shop, Mama and I. Papa had not yet returned home from the university.

We ate our ice-cream cones, teeter-tottered in the park, walked all around Brookline. When we got back home, Mama quietly unlocked the door, like the time before, quietly turned the knob. The lights flickered on just as she shut the door. It happened suddenly, Papa coming at us, dark and looming, like a shadow.

'I get home and there's no dinner,' he shouted. 'Now that you're in America, you think you can behave like an American, staying out all hours of the night?'

Mama shook her head frantically, mumbled something about having lost track of time.

'Lost track of time?' he asked. His hand came down on her. Once. Twice. The third time, I got in the way, tried to stop him. His hand came down on me.

'Is it the effect America is having on you?' he shouted. 'Did you ever lose track of time like this in Nigeria? No! All of a sudden you're losing track! I'll teach you a lesson on losing track of time. I'll teach you both.'

More hands on us, pounding and pounding until we were down on our knees, crouched by the door, trying to catch our breath. Then the lights flickered off. We remained on the floor. We fell asleep there, Mama's arms wrapped around me.

She must have called the next morning, after Papa left for the university, after I left for school.

Later, in the afternoon, I was sitting on the floor of my bedroom, sheets of homework scattered across the floor. Papa had not yet returned.

Mama said, 'Hurry. We have an appointment to keep.' I wondered what exactly the appointment was for.

We used to straighten our hair with those thick metal combs back then, the kind without electric cords, the kinds you stuck on top of one of the burners of a gas stove, on top of the blue-and-orange flames. You'd leave the comb sitting there on the fire while you parted the hair into sections. When you were done parting, and when the comb was nice and hot, steaming even, you'd pick it up, blow a little on it with your mouth, just to blow off a little of the steam. Then you'd stretch the hair with the comb, piece by piece, until there was not a single kinky curl left on the entire head.

I found her standing in front of the kitchen. I could see the stretching comb where it lay, on an open flame behind her.

'Five minutes,' she said. 'Run into the bathroom, wash your face, brush your teeth, and change into one of your Sunday dresses, something nice.'

The dress I chose was my best one, the purple dress from the Salvation Army on Mass Ave, with the white polka dots and red ribbon in front. The seams were just starting to come apart at the sides, and under one arm a small hole had formed. No one could have seen the hole, so I put on the dress. And afterwards I went into the kitchen, where Mama was still standing by the stove, the stretching comb sticking out purposefully from her hand.

'Mama, where are we going?' I asked.

No response.

'Mama, did you hear me?'

'Turn your head this way.'

As soon as she finished with me, she put on her own dress. Not the adire wrappers she used to wear in Nigeria, no fancy headscarves like the ones she used to tie. Nothing special, just one of those long beige dresses, fraying at the hem, but still one of the nicer ones that she wore to church on Sundays. An American dress. It was the beginning of fall by now, but all around people were still wearing dresses.

Soon we were walking out the door.

Out in the courtyard little Christophine was chasing her

big sister Lexine, trying to get the ball that Lexine held in her hands. Romain and Stefon sat on the steps that led down to the courtyard, exchanging cards and candy bars.

Shruti stood up from where she was sitting on the railing of the steps. We were the same age, Shruti and I, and in the same homeroom – Mrs Stephen's class. Every afternoon, she waited for me. We played together until dinner time. That was the way it was those days. A building of all international students, Indians, Africans, Caribbean mostly. We'd all come out in the late afternoons and we'd play until sunset, until our mothers or our fathers came to call us in.

Shruti followed Mama and me. 'When will you be back?' she asked. She walked alongside us, her dupatta carelessly strewn across her body, one end sweeping the floor. 'Will you be back soon?'

'Maybe,' Mama answered.

'Maybe,' I echoed.

At the tip of the road, that junction where Buswell Street intersected Beacon Street, Mama stopped, and I stopped, too, and we stood watching the cars pass by, waiting to cross. Shruti stood with us, a disappointed look on her face.

'You should get back now,' Mama said, not turning to look at Shruti. 'You should get back before your mother starts to worry.'

Of course, Shruti obeyed.

We crossed the street then, continued to walk, past Tony's Pizza shop, up to and past Kenmore Square, where Emmanuel College and Simmons College and all the other colleges formed their little community. We trekked on, side by side, Mama holding my hand. All of it we did in silence.

It was Mama who finally broke the silence. She began slowly and softly, marvelling at how wonderful it was that there were things like churches, food banks and nice people who worked in both. 'Everything so organized.'

I listened.

'Who would have known that there were places where people could go to have these types of problems solved?' she asked. Places that were not churches, not food banks, not hospitals. But they were actually a sort of hospital, she said. Then, 'Ah, what a country!' What a country it was that had exactly what a person needed, if only the person knew enough to ask. She hadn't even known that she could ask, she said. But somehow God had put it in her mind. And thank Heaven she did. Because things would surely get better from here. It would not be like in Nigeria where everyone had insisted that it was her duty to remain with Papa.

We stopped by the tram and got on. Mama held my hand the entire ride. It might have been a thing she did only to steady herself, because her hand shook each time that she loosened her grasp on mine.

We got off at Copley Station. More walking. Past the public library, past Boylston Street. Past block after block of houses. We stopped when we came to a street of row houses.

Mama pulled out the card, the one the woman had given to her. I was surprised by its relative crispness, how even with all this passage of time, it appeared well preserved, not at all as I would have expected, for having been buried so long inside of Mama's bag.

I stared at it. Mama stared at it too, for a few seconds, as if surprised by it the way that I was.

The house at which we arrived had a wooden red door and a wooden plate posted at Mama's eye level. Painted on the plate was a pink triangle without a base, and underneath the triangle, the words FRESH START.

As we stood in front of the door, Mama turned to me, rubbed her hand on my cheeks, as if wiping off any dirt that had accrued from the trip. She fussed a bit with my hair, tucking the straightened strands into place. She fussed with the skirt of my dress, straightened it out. Perhaps wrinkles had formed during the trip, and if so, she made sure to remove all traces of them. Only then did she knock.

A woman opened the door, pretty, with pale skin and dark brown hair that came down to her shoulders. She wore an expensive-looking blouse, something shiny, like silk. Her skirt came down just below her knees, perfectly ironed, perfectly tailored, nothing like Mama's old, fraying dress.

She invited us inside and offered us seats at her desk.

The room was wide, with posters on the walls, of mothers and children, of families with smiling faces. There were other types of posters, too, of purple ribbons and bold letters that read: STOP DOMESTIC VIOLENCE.

I exhaled – one of those lengthy exhales that seemed to tumble on and on, whose end you were eager to reach, because somehow it held the promise of something good. I exhaled, and I settled comfortably into my seat.

Soft music came from somewhere. There were also sounds from above, of feet and of children's hushed voices.

On the main floor, where we were, there were two other women like Mama, each one sitting at one of the three desks in the room.

One woman had two sons; they appeared to be twins, perhaps about three or four years old. They gathered around her lap, each one resting his head on a thigh.

At the other desk was a woman with her daughter. She sat filling out, I suppose, the same forms Mama was filling out for us. The woman's daughter sat quietly, her hair in pigtails.

A widescreen television sat in the corner of the room, muted, alternating between news and weather reports. No broken antenna sticking up above it, not like our television, its antenna having been chopped off by Papa in one of his fits of anger.

The chairs were nice and cushioned – nothing new, but without the holes that ours had at home. And no broken legs, like some of ours had come to have after so many instances of Papa throwing them into the wall.

It was a good place, I thought. Fancy television, nice furnishings, mostly quiet. No Papa to worry about.

The woman helping Mama had been speaking all the while, but I had been too busy observing my surroundings to hear what exactly she was saying. Now, I listened closely, and I heard. She had handed over a clipboard to Mama. On the clipboard was a form. She was instructing Mama on which blanks to fill on the form.

Mama was still filling out the forms when another woman came down the staircase from upstairs.

She was the same woman from the night at the bus stop. The same woman from our visits to the food bank at our church on Buswell Street.

She patted me on the head. She looked at Mama, told her how happy she was that we had come. Her eyes were soft, a little tired-looking.

'You'll be safe here,' she said. It could have been to me or to Mama.

Mama nodded, then continued to fill out the forms.

The woman walked across to the other two desks, appearing to check in with the mothers and children. She checked in also with the counsellors at the desks before turning around and going back upstairs.

We waited. Our counsellor made some calls. We waited some more. Intermittently, Mama rubbed my shoulders, told me how all this was really for the best. It was not as if she needed to convince me of it. I had begun imagining evenings at the place, imagining that those noises I was hearing upstairs were voices of children my age. After five or six o'clock, when the counsellors went home, I imagined that all the kids came down the stairs, like we did in our Buswell Street apartment building, all the children gathering together in the hours before dinner. Here, we'd gather around that widescreen television and watch our choice of movies.

I was thinking all this as the woman from the bus stop approached us again. She stood by Mama's side, shaking her head from side to side. At first she did not say a thing.

'What?' Mama asked, finally.

Our counsellor stood leaning on her desk, just watching, her eyes going between Mama and the woman.

'Is something the matter?' Mama asked.

A pause. 'Your husband,' the woman responded, like a question.

'He doesn't know,' Mama said, answering what she assumed was the question. 'You won't need to tell him, will you?'

The woman shook her head. 'He would only know what you allowed him to know,' she said. 'But that's not the problem.' Silence. 'Your husband,' the woman tried again. 'He's a student?'

Mama nodded. 'Engineering,' she said. 'Boston University.'

'He is here on a student visa?' the counsellor asked.

Again, Mama nodded.

Then the woman was shaking her head once more, telling Mama how sorry she was. A slip of her mind, she said. It was something she should have done, but that evening by the bus stop, all she had thought was of the swollen lips, of all the bruises she'd seen on us over the past few months. It had somehow not occurred to her to ask what papers we had. It had not occurred to her that day to inquire about the status of our residency.

'It complicates things,' she said, still shaking her head. 'But basically, I'm afraid there's not much I can do given the situation.' Surely we still had family back in Nigeria. Couldn't we simply return home to them, and leave Papa here to finish his studies on his own? There was that look on the woman's face as she spoke, an almost blank stare, as if she knew, as we did, that that solution was as good as no solution at all.

Mama remained silent, listening, or maybe no longer listening. Maybe trying to readjust her mind, like I was, to the idea that we would be returning to Papa.

I looked into the woman's eyes, big and blue, which reminded me again of E.T. Of course, she would actually have been more like Elliot or Gertie or Michael. We had somehow become stranded in her country, and she'd have loved to hide us in the closet the way that they'd all hidden E.T. She'd have helped us, would have taken care of us. Only, somehow, she couldn't.

We walked down the street, past the row houses, climbed into the tram, climbed off the tram, all in silence. It was not until we turned the corner on Buswell Street that Mama finally spoke. 'She's a nice lady,' she said.

I nodded.

'She tried,' Mama said.

I nodded.

'Maybe things will get better with your papa,' she said.

'Maybe,' I said. We climbed down the stairs leading to the courtyard of our building, and I imagined E.T., sick and weak, lying helpless on the bathroom floor. That was partly the way the movie would have ended that evening long ago, if I had watched it to the end. Government agents invading the house. Then E.T. on that hospital-looking bed, all those masked scientists, dressed in white, trying to nurse him back to health. The children on their bicycles flying into the sunset, then landing back on the ground. The children staring expectantly at the greying sky, watching and waiting for E.T's people to land and carry him back home.

Grace

The first time I see her, she is crouched by the entrance of the third-floor bathroom, at an equal distance between my office and the lecture hall where I teach. She is sobbing, and her shoulders are shaking slightly, so I stop, crouch down to be closer to her level, pat her on the shoulder and ask her if she's all right. She nods and mumbles something under her breath. Then she lifts her head, wipes away tears with her hands and smiles at me, a weak smile. 'I'm okay,' she says. Her voice is faint and comes out like a croak. There is a pause, and then another croak. I'm not sure what she says that second time around, but the sound makes me think of frogs, small and slimy, of Exodus and the second plague, of the inundation of the Nile, of Pharaoh and his magicians challenging God by creating more frogs. I think of all this because that's what's on my mind these days. That's what I teach that semester. The Old Testament.

I straighten up and look in the direction of my office. There is a yellow cart in the centre of the hallway, and not too far from the cart, a janitor is pushing a tall broom across the floor. There is a clock hanging from the ceiling on the far end of the hallway. I look at it and then I look back down at her. 'It's about 5 p.m.,' I say. 'They'll be locking up the building very soon.'

She nods and lifts herself up from the floor. She is clutching a handbag to her chest, grasping it as if it is some kind of life support, and then all of a sudden she starts to bawl so hard that she seems to be gasping for air. I start again to pat her on the shoulder, and somehow I find myself leading her back to my office, pulling out a seat for her, one of the two seats in the room that are reserved for my students. Except I'm not even sure that she's a student of mine. And in my twenty years at the university, I've never seen any of them weep like this before.

'I'm sorry,' I say to her, because I truly am sorry to see her crying so hard. She leans forward on the chair, still clasping her bag, rocking it and herself back and forth. Slowly her sobbing declines until I can only hear the occasional catch of her breath. She rises from her seat and heads for the door.

'If you ever need someone to talk to—' I say. I don't finish.

At the doorway, she turns to look at me. 'Thanks,' she says, and as she says it, I allow my eyes to linger on her. I look at her braids – thin, black braids that extend down past her shoulders. I observe the tone of her skin – a dark olive complexion, unique in its hue. Her lips are swollen and reddish, and there are streaks of tears staining her cheeks. I wonder where exactly she is from. As she walks out the door, I find myself thinking what a shame it is that anybody should be made to cry that much.

A few days go by – Thursday, Friday and the weekend. I've almost forgotten the crying incident by Monday when I step into the lecture hall for my Old Testament class. The class itself is a different demographic than other graduate courses I've taught, say, Chaucer, or Milton, or even my Greek Mythology class. These students are more zealous than any I've had before. I figure that maybe it's the Bible's effect on things. Or maybe it's a consequence of age, because from the look of things, most of these students are in their thirties and forties, older than my typical set of students. And, unlike former students, these ones are quite fond of scheduling meetings with me. They do it with such alarming frequency that at certain points in the semester,

I go back and forth about whether to put a cap on the number of visits allowed per student. Not because I don't want to meet with them, but because after a while, I get tired of hearing the same questions over and over again, questions like why the books of the Old Testament are organized the way they are, or why it is that in Leviticus God bans cripples from approaching his altar. Often enough, my answer is that it's a good question, but that there are several possibilities, all of which are subject to debate.

In any case, I step into the lecture hall, and a group of my students walks in the door with me, making small talk about God and the weather. I nod and smile at the things they say, and after we enter, I head directly to the front of the room, the way I always do. I jot down some Bible verses on the board, write some notes about apodictic law versus casuistic law, about Hammurabi's Code versus the Ten Commandments, about goodness for goodness' sake versus goodness with an eye to some type of reward or punishment. I wipe the chalk off my hands and turn around to face the class, and I catch a glimpse of her, the girl with the long black braids, sitting in the corner at the very back of the room. I smile. She looks down. I figure she's still a bit embarrassed about the crying, so I go on with the lecture, and I try not to look her way again.

After class, I'm packing up my notes, stuffing my Bible into my bag, when I hear her.

'Excuse me,' she says. 'I'm Grace.'

She asks me when my office hours are. I tell her. Thursday mornings, 9 a.m. to 12 noon. She nods. I smile. She doesn't smile back. She says, 'I'd like to come in and talk to you about the Bible.'

'Sure,' I say. No surprise there. That's all they're coming in to talk to me about this semester.

Before she turns around, I notice the seriousness of her face. There is something tragic and vulnerable about her look. I think how such seriousness should be accompanied by a fine set of wrinkles across the forehead, or around the eyes and mouth. But she is young.

She turns to leave, and I notice the way her braids hang down past her shoulders. Something about the way they move as she walks makes me want to reach out and touch them, but I remain where I am and watch her walk out of the room. And I think that there couldn't be a more fitting name for her.

On Thursday, I'm sitting in my office with my door cracked open, flipping through my stack of mail, when she knocks on the door. I invite her in, and she shuts the door behind her. They sometimes do, when what they have to talk to me about is personal.

I take in her face again – that startling combination of youth and old age. Her clothes are even an extension of that paradox: a white dress shirt, buttoned almost to the very top, prudishly, though I can see the outline of her bra from the white, diaphanous cotton. She has tucked the bottom of the blouse into the waistline of her greyish skirt. On her feet, she wears a pair of simple leather slippers. The only jewellery she wears is a pair of pearl earrings. A very neat presentation, which makes me aware of my own not-so-tidy look. I tug the hem of my untucked shirt, as if tugging will straighten out the wrinkles on it. I fuss with my earrings, and I'm grateful that I even remembered them today. I run my fingers through my hair and hope that I catch and put back into place any stray hairs. I cross my legs under the table and ask her to take a seat.

She is holding her Bible, a small King James with a maroon

cover, and all over the inside are pink and yellow Post-it notes, as if she's been doing some very serious research.

She tells me that she only has a few questions. That they are probably silly questions, but that she would like to see what I think, since I'm the only Bible researcher she knows from a strictly academic background. I'll probably give her a different take on things than she's used to getting, she says. I notice that she speaks with a bit of an accent, barely perceptible, just enough that I know she's probably from somewhere as unique as her looks. I nod.

She quotes me 2 Timothy: 'All scripture is given inspiration by God, and is profitable for doctrine, for reproof, for correction, for instruction in righteousness.' She asks me, how exactly do we know that God has inspired the Bible? Because the Bible has caused quite a bit of destruction in the world, she says. How do we really know that God even approves of some of the things in the Bible?

I smile and tell her, 'Sorry, I'm only dealing with the Old Testament this semester. Timothy is the New Testament.' I start to laugh, because it's meant to be a joke, but her face is thoughtful and disappointed, so I clear my throat, and I apologize for the joke.

I tell her that religion is all about faith. And one's faith is a very personal thing.

She tells me that there are things in the Bible that could not possibly be from God, contradictions like the whole idea of God being a god of peace, but also a god of war. 'Which one is it?' she asks. And what about love your neighbour as yourself, and yet God forbids the cripples from approaching his altar? What kind of God bans the very creatures he created from coming to him just because of imperfections out of their control?

I tell her that she needs to keep in mind that the Bible was written under a certain cultural context. It is inspired by God in many ways, but it was still written by humans, with human biases, all based on the existing cultural norms of the time.

She nods and says, 'So if humans are making their own rules, and writing the rules down in the Bible, where exactly does the Godly inspiration come into play?'

'Well,' I say, 'God inspired them to set down the rules in the first place. And when you look at all the ancient books in the world, none have lasted as long and have had as much influence as the Bible. That in itself is an attestation to some kind of divine inspiration, I think.'

'I suppose,' she says. 'But then how do we know what rules are God's and what rules are man's? I need to know,' she says.

'Give an example,' I say. 'Are you worried about any particular rule?'

'Like divorce,' she says. 'Is it adultery to divorce and remarry, or is it permissible? And shouldn't it at least depend on the specific circumstance? What about in the case of an abusive husband? Must the woman stay?'

I hesitate a bit. I wonder if she's contemplating divorce, or if she's just picking out an example. Then I think of my own divorce, nearly fifteen years ago now. I remember the loneliness of it all, the disappointment in failing at something as important as marriage. 'Marriage is a sacred union,' I say, even as I'm reminiscing about my own marriage. 'When something happens that makes the union no longer sacred, I believe that is grounds enough for divorce.'

'But is the Bible okay with that?' she asks. 'Is God okay with that?'

'I don't know,' I say. 'It's difficult to know.'

We stay quiet for a while. Then I look up at her. There is a trail of tears coming down one side of her face. The other side is still winning the battle, resisting the tears.

'I'm sorry my class is upsetting you this much,' I say.

'No,' she says. 'It's not your class.' She wipes her tears away. 'I'm sorry about all this crying,' she says.

'Don't be sorry,' I say.

She looks up at me, then she looks down at her Bible, flips it open. 'Thou shall not lie with mankind as with womankind: it is an abomination.' She pauses. 'If a man also lie with mankind, as he lieth with a woman, both of them have committed an abomination: they shall surely be put to death.'

I'm intrigued by the verses she reads. All of a sudden the conversation is taking a different turn. I remain quiet and simply listen to see where it'll go.

'Does this also apply to females?' she asks. 'Is it also an abomination for women to lie with women?'

Aha, I think. 'It's a tricky one,' I say. 'Try not to take it all so literally. There are things in the Bible that should not be taken literally.'

'I don't understand,' she says.

'Like the word "abomination",' I say. 'It's hard to even know what that meant back then. Meanings change over time. It's hard to know.'

She looks down at her Bible, and I know that she's seriously considering everything that I've said. She says, 'It's hard to know right from wrong, especially when some things feel right, and yet there are so many people telling you how wrong they are.'

I nod. Usually I'm listening to questions that don't have to do with anything personal. Just demonstrations of intellect and scholarship. I want to hug her and tell her that one day she'll figure it out for herself. But I'm not so sure of that, and so I don't move. Instead I say, 'The greatest commandments, according to Jesus, are, first, love the Lord your God with all your heart and soul and mind. And second, love your neighbour as yourself.'

She looks up at me, and I smile at her. She smiles back. On her way out she tells me thank you for the talk.

'Any time,' I say.

Two weeks later, I'm sitting in my office, my back to the door, when I think I hear a knock so soft that I have to turn around to check if someone is really there. From the opening, I can see a bit of her face, standing by, waiting for me to answer.

I pull open the door, invite her in. She is holding a white paper bag in one hand and a card and envelope in another. She tells me she's brought something for me. She sits down, signs the card in front of me, and as she's signing it, she's muttering something about my having to excuse her cursive, because she never really learned how to write in cursive. I ask her why. She looks up at me, all thoughtful, and says, 'They didn't teach cursive in Nigeria.' She puts her head back down and continues to write.

I say, 'Oh, I would have thought maybe it's because of your age or something. I don't believe they're still teaching it in schools these days. I don't believe they've taught it for at least a couple of decades now. Probably they wouldn't have been teaching it for people your age, even if you were in America.'

She looks back up at me and smiles. 'I'm not so young,' she says, handing me the card.

'Does it say something sweet?' I ask, and immediately I'm embarrassed by the question, because I realize that I'm not only hoping that it does, but that I'm also voicing my desire to her.

'Not really,' she says. 'But what it says should be good enough.'

I feel the heat rise in my face. I tell her thank you. She gets up, tells me to have a good day. She leaves the room.

In class the next week, I keep from looking her way and I'm not sure exactly why.

Another week passes by, and then she comes back to my office. It's the same routine each time, and it repeats every other week or so. She knocks on my door, peeks in and asks me how I am. I tell her fine. She says, 'Good.' And then she wishes me a good rest of the day and leaves.

Thanksgiving comes and goes, and we all start to wrap ourselves up with thick scarves and wool mittens.

The last week before Christmas break she knocks on my door, and I tell her to come in. She is wearing a brown hat, some kind of knit, and half her face is wrapped up with a matching scarf. She enters the room, closes the door behind her, raises her hands to her face to remove the scarf, and it's only then that I realize she's upset – and quite a bit angry even, which results in a look that I've not until then seen on her face.

I stand up and wrap my arms around her. 'Somehow it all works out,' I say. I used to tell this to myself during my divorce, and weeks afterwards. Then the weeks turned into months, and months into years. And I found myself chanting it less.

She mumbles something about letters, about her mother. Then she stays silent for a while, and I feel her body gently relax into mine.

'It'll be all right,' I say, my arms still wrapped around her. She exhales.

We stay like that for some time, and then I loosen my hold on her, allow my hands to drop to her waist. Her hands also make their way down to my waist.

She tells me then, her voice faint and contemplative, that she was the one who signed for the packet the day the first batch of letters came, nearly a year ago now. She starts to laugh, softly, as if she's suddenly in a trance, but then she stops with the laugh and continues to speak. She tells me that the forecasts that day called for snow, but the delivery man only wore a shirt – the standard yellow-and-red polo, with its red collar and red hem around the sleeves. She tells me that the colour pattern of the shirt matched that of his van, yellow and red all over again. He wore a hat, she says, which, when he removed it, revealed a head of greying hair. She looks at me. 'Salt and pepper like yours,' she says. 'He had blue eyes, too,' she continues. 'Only not as beautiful as yours.' She stops awkwardly then and looks down as if suddenly embarrassed or shy.

Our hands are still around each other's waists, and there is only a little space between us, and suddenly I have this image in my head of John Rosenberg making out in his office with that female student of his. I don't remember who it was that walked in on them, but I know he lost his tenure that way, created a scandal in the department that lasted quite a while.

It occurs to me that if someone were to walk into my office at that very moment, things between Grace and me would appear inappropriate. I've never consoled a student like this before. And with my closest family members half the country away, in Massachusetts, it's been a while since I stood this close to anyone, excepting a few cursory hugs with friends and co-workers. It occurs to me that I should take my hands off her waist, but I don't, and, thinking back now, the reason I don't is quite clear. But at that very moment, all I am thinking is that I prefer to leave my hands where they are, and that, anyway, it couldn't possibly be inappropriate, being that I'm a woman, and she's a woman, and I'm probably older than her mother.

She continues to tell me about the DHL man. How he

handed her the yellow package with a smile on his face. Always
the same delivery man, she tells me, with the same truck, DHL
printed on it and Worldwide Express underneath the DHL.
She tells me that she thought she knew what the package
was, some silly correspondence for her mother from Nigeria,
because silly correspondences were often coming for her
mother from Nigeria.

'Did I tell you I have a brother?' she asks suddenly, her hands
letting go of my waist.

'No,' I say, also letting go.

She nods. 'Arinze,' she says. 'Five years older than I am.
When we were little, he and I used to take turns climbing a
stool that my mother kept in the attic. It was our playroom,
that attic room,' she says. I wonder why she is telling me this,
but I don't ask. Instead, I pull out a seat for her and then one
for me. We both sit.

'It only had one window,' she continues, 'which was so near
the ceiling that we had to climb on the stool to open it up.'

She tells me that my office reminds her a bit of the attic
room, with its exposed brick walls, with the tiny holes between
the bricks. She says something about millipedes and centipedes
crawling out of the holes in the summer and the spring. It all
comes out like something in between a statement and a question, and I wonder if she's asking me about my office or telling
me about her mama's attic.

'But it's been years since either of us used the stool,' she
says. 'Years since either of us opened or closed the window.
Which explains the smell,' she says. 'Building up and then
settling into every corner, into every item in every corner
of the room. The scent of mothballs, and of Mentholatum.' She
laughs softly again, shaking her head as she does. Then she tells
me that she's wrong. That my office is nothing like the attic,

because even though there are the brick walls and the tiny holes, the scent is missing. 'It's a good thing,' she says.

I nod and say, 'Okay.'

'I handed the envelope to Mama,' she says. And she tells me everything in so much detail that I can see their kitchen in my head and I can see her mama sitting on the short stool, her legs wrapped around the circumference of the mortar, pounding yam with the pestle. 'All this time in America,' she says. 'And still, Mama must pound her yam in the mortar, the good old-fashioned way.'

'How long have you been in America?' I ask.

'Years,' she says. 'Just over twelve years now.' She came around age eleven, she tells me. I do the math and am a bit disappointed to find out that she's barely in her mid-twenties.

She breathes deeply and continues. 'I walk into the kitchen and hand the envelope to Mama,' she says. 'Meanwhile Arinze is downstairs, I can hear the hammering and the drilling. He is putting together a shelf for Mama. Always stopping by, helping Mama around the house, fixing or putting together something for her. A perfect son, really,' she says. 'Which is why Mama put him in charge of managing her stores, coordinating the shipments of the products from Nigeria, that sort of thing.'

I nod, trying to follow along. But mostly I suppose that I nod just out of gratitude that she is still there by my side, gratitude that she is sitting so close to me.

'There was a whole batch of letters in the envelope,' she says. 'And this time they weren't for Mama,' she says. 'They were all for me.'

'From whom?' I ask.

'Men,' she says. 'Marriage proposals.' Her voice begins to break, and something in my stomach takes a plunge. I tell myself that it's because I don't want to watch her cry again.

'Do you know the men?' I ask.

She shakes her head and then leans it on my shoulder. I can feel the roughness of her braids rubbing on my jaw. And her scent is fleshy but sweet.

'There's one,' she says. 'Nwafor.' She lifts her head. 'An Igbo man who lives in the Lekki district of Lagos, in one of those big houses with uniformed gatemen. Owns his own accounting firm.' She pauses. 'Mama likes that part,' she says. 'The part about owning his own business. And she likes that he really wants to marry me,' she says.

She tells me that his letters are filled with things like, 'You're the wife of my dreams, my African queen.' She pauses, then she exclaims, 'How silly it is for Mama to expect me to marry a man I've only seen in pictures!'

I ask her if he has seen her, if he has any idea what she looks like, or is he just operating under some kind of divine guidance?

She tells me, yes, that he's seen her picture. That her mama took the picture herself, that her mama placed the stool by the empty wall of the dining room and forced her to sit there. Her mama arranged her braids so that they framed her face and shoulders just so. She rubbed some maroon lip gloss on her lips, and lent her a pair of gold-and-pearl chandelier earrings. Then she snapped the picture, over and over again, until finally she got the one that she said was just right. This was the only picture of her that Nwafor saw, as far as she knew. Somehow, she tells me – and she can't even begin to understand how – it was exactly what he needed to make the decision to marry her.

I rub her shoulders and tell her that I'm sorry. 'Has a date been set?' I ask.

'I don't know,' she says. She tells me how it was just the

beginning of this semester that Nwafor made the official request to her mother, in a letter. And, of course, her mother said yes, told her that it was all for the best. Any girl would be a fool to decline a man who wanted her as much as Nwafor wanted her. All of this, she tells me, happened the day that I found her by the entrance to the bathroom.

I ask her what's been going on since then.

'Just waiting,' she says. 'And praying that Nwafor or Mama would have a change of heart.'

I say, 'No luck, I take it.'

She shakes her head. 'No luck,' she says. She tells me that this morning she finally got the courage to say something to her mother. That she walked down the hallway in their house, climbed up the stairs and into the attic, because her mama was there, sorting piles of paper, maybe business papers. She says to her mama, 'I'm not marrying him.' I imagine her mama hunched over on the ground, and then slowly straightening up, a pair of glasses hanging on the bridge of her nose. At first she doesn't respond to Grace. And then she clears her throat, or adjusts her glasses, whatever the appropriate tick. 'Stop that nonsense,' she finally says.

And then her brother Arinze walks into the attic room, holding a box, the one into which she assumes her mother will be sorting the piles of paper.

'Mama, I'm not getting married,' Grace says.

Her mother goes back to not responding, so Grace raises her voice and says, 'Did you hear me, Mama?'

'She's not deaf,' Arinze says.

'Mama?' Grace says, softer.

Her mother still does not answer.

Grace tells me that suddenly her mama speaks again, all serious and threatening. 'All that studying,' her mother says.

'You'll marry your studies? Marry your books? You already have one degree but you want another. You'll marry your degrees?'

This time it's Grace who does not answer.

'Am I talking to the wall?' her mama asks. 'Answer me!' And then she doesn't wait for an answer. She says, 'Before you know it, you'll look around and find yourself all alone, just you and your degrees. And then what?'

She tells her mama then that it's not for her.

'What's not for you?' her mama asks.

'Marriage,' she says.

'Marriage is not for you?' her mama scoffs. 'Your papa, God rest his soul, would cringe in his grave if he heard you say such nonsense. What good is having that doctorate that you're going for, if your life is empty – no husband, no children?'

'It's not for me,' she tells her mama again. But she doesn't tell her mama the entire truth. It's not the marriage part that's not for her. It's the fact that she doesn't like men in the marrying way. She's never been interested in them like that. She tells me this now, though, truth be told, I think I already knew.

'A woman needs to marry, have children,' her mama says. 'Life is more satisfying that way.'

'She'll marry her books and degrees,' Arinze says, chuckling.

'Shut up,' she tells her brother, in a whisper.

'You shut up,' Arinze says. 'And better watch how you talk to me, old maid.'

'Be quiet,' her mama says to her. 'You'll get married. That's final,' she says, and she returns to the piles of papers that she is sorting.

Grace then turns to leave the attic room, but something makes her turn back. So she stands facing her mama. She fixes her eyes on one of the holes on the brick wall. She takes in slow, calculated breaths to steady herself. Then she says, calmly, in a clear, firm voice, 'I won't.'

Suddenly her mama is slapping her, saying something about defiance. And she is screaming, and her mama is screaming too. She is trying to push her mama away, and then she feels Arinze towering above her, pounding his fists down on her shoulders. 'Don't you dare disrespect Mama like that!' he shouts. 'Don't you dare!' More pounding. She struggles to breathe, but every breath by then is suffocating, saturated with the scent of moth-balls, and of undiluted Mentholatum. And then the brick walls in the room start spinning around her, and her shoulders are throbbing, because she is now down on her knees, she tells me, and still Arinze's fists are pounding down on her.

'I can't take it any more,' she finishes, like a sigh. I can see the tears in her eyes. I sit there and allow her to lean her head once more against my shoulder.

Before she leaves, I mention the counselling services at the university. I ask her if she's ever been there. She shakes her head. I tell her that perhaps someone there can help her more than I can. She shakes her head again. 'Try it out,' I say, trying to sound adamant. 'At least think about it,' I say. But even as I say it, there is a part of me that wishes she won't, because there's the possibility that if she finds the counselling people more helpful than me, she might begin to rely wholly on them and stop coming to me.

That night, I take a walk around town. Christmas lights hang above every doorway, and the ground is covered with snow. The air is cold and feels as if it is pricking the skin on my cheeks. I imagine pins and needles, and thin, rusting metal wires, poking my skin. I tell myself that perhaps this is my punishment, for these new thoughts, these inappropriate desires. All the same, I tug at my scarf and my hat, adjusting them so that they both come together to cover the exposed portions of my face.

There is a strong hazelnut aroma in the air, which I follow instinctively. It leads me to a coffee shop, Brewed Awakenings. Even with the cold, the scent is so strong and oddly appeasing, like a balm, that for a moment I consider stopping to buy myself a cup of coffee, even if coffee is not my thing, has never been. But I don't. Instead, I take a seat at one of the benches a short distance from the tall glass window. And I breathe in the aroma. And I watch the people inside.

There is a couple sitting by the window. They are wearing hats, and they have muffled themselves up with oversized scarves that appear more like cloaks. Then he removes his hat and removes his cloak, and she does the same. He smiles at her, reaches out and stirs the contents of her cup while she is still struggling to take off her gloves. Their hands come together, his dark on her fair skin, and I think of Grace, and I imagine Nwafor putting his hand on her. And then the woman takes her cup, takes a sip out of it, and she laughs at something he says. She looks happy, and I find myself hoping that Nwafor will make Grace happy like that. So long as she is happy, I say to myself. And I find myself trying hard to remember if I've ever heard of or read about or watched any stories in which an arranged marriage ends up being successful. Of course the only examples that come to my mind are from the Bible. I think of Isaac, how Abraham asks his servant to go find a wife for him. And that woman ends up being Rebekah. And the servant asks her father for permission to take Rebekah back home to Isaac. And her parents give the permission. She does not know what Isaac looks like, neither does Isaac know what she looks like. And yet the marriage ensues and for all intents and purposes appears to be a success. Of course, the big difference is that Rebekah *agrees* to marry Isaac.

'Will you go with this man?' they ask her.

'I will go,' she says.

Just a few days before Christmas, my daughter calls me from Massachusetts, tells me that because of a mix-up in plans, they will be spending this Christmas with her in-laws, that they will no longer be coming down to be with me. It's been this way since my grandson was born, three Christmases now, and each time she comes up with a similar excuse. She tells me it has to be done because her husband's family will be very upset if they don't make it.

'What about me?' I ask.

She says, 'Mom, it's just you. He's got the whole family, brothers, sisters, aunts, uncles, cousins. They'll all be angry with me. Please understand,' she says. 'I'll make it up to you. In the meantime, better for one person to be mad at me than the whole gang.'

I tell her fine, that I anyway have research to do and lectures to prepare. And the truth is that I'd much rather not be dealing with the chaos of family Christmases, all those people gathered in one small space, and not in an orderly fashion, as in a lecture hall. Still, it'd be nice to bake pies and prepare the meal together, to chit-chat and catch up as we do. It'd also be nice not to have to eat alone, because these days, maybe as a result of the Christmas season, or the cold weather, I'm feeling lonelier than ever, and eating has begun to feel like a chore, a solitary task without any enjoyment in it. Even so, I tell my daughter, 'Fine.' She thanks me hastily and hangs up the phone.

I immerse myself in work the entire break, but between the research and the preparation for lectures and conferences, I find myself thinking of Grace. I think of the feel of her braids on my skin and of her smile. I remember her collared dress and her musty perfumed scent. And every now and then there is a feeling of dread when I think of the possibility that she will be a married woman the next time I see her.

The New Year arrives, and then a week later, classes resume. The first week, I don't see Grace. The second week, I'm sure she will show up, but she doesn't. I begin to mope about. Every passing day becomes a great disappointment, though there are those brief moments of hope, moments where I find myself recognizing Grace's features in another young woman. But then the young woman turns around and I see that it's not her. And I'm left feeling even emptier than before.

The third week, sitting in my office, flipping through the pages of the New Testament, I hear the knock. She enters without my inviting her in. I'm expecting that she will head straight to one of the two empty seats. Instead she stops near me. My front is facing my desk, and my back is to her, so she simply hugs me from behind before taking a seat. She apologizes for being gone all this time, for returning so late into the semester. She asks me if I had a good Christmas break, and all I can do is nod.

She stretches out her hand to stroke my arm. 'I'm sorry,' she says. Maybe the look on my face somehow tells her how miserable I've been.

I look down at my arm, at her hand on it. She retracts it, shyly, as if she's suddenly aware of an indiscretion. I want to tell her that I've been thinking of her, but instead I find myself saying, 'Are you married now?'

She looks curiously at me, and for a moment I feel as if I am trespassing, as if the question is not mine to ask. But her curious glance quickly fades away, and she shakes her head and tells me 'No,' but that soon she will be. This time it is I who reaches out and strokes her arm.

'It's okay,' she says. 'It's not the end of the world.'

'Isn't it?' I ask, wanting her to tell me that it is in fact the end of the world, wanting her to begin crying so that I can hold her again.

She shakes her head. She says, 'No.' Then she clears her throat. 'I'd like you to come,' she says.

'To your wedding?' I ask.

She nods.

I shake my head and tell her I can't. That I'll probably be at a lecture somewhere. But that even if I weren't, there'd be no reason for me to attend her wedding, given that I'm just her professor.

'Really?' she asks.

'Really,' I say, forcing myself to stick to the excuse.

We both stare at each other for some time. Neither of us speaks. Then she says, 'I was in Nigeria over the break.'

'Really?' I ask.

She nods.

She tells me how it was sort of in preparation for her own wedding, because her cousin Ogechukwu was getting married, and her mama wanted her to attend the wedding ceremonies – the traditional and the white – to remind her first-hand how authentic Nigerian weddings were done, so that she would know what was expected of her in her own wedding.

She stops there, and when she doesn't continue, all I can think to ask is whether or not her brother or her mother went with her.

She nods. 'Mama went with me,' she says. 'Not Arinze,' she says. Because, she tells me, according to her Mama, Arinze already knew the culture, already knew what it meant to be Nigerian. It was she who caused her mama some concern.

She tells me her mama is right. That sometimes she barely feels Nigerian, which she knows has never been the case with Arinze. Growing up, Arinze was always speaking Igbo with her mama while she could only understand and respond in English. Arinze would always swallow his balls of garri after dipping them into the soup. She, on the other hand, chewed hers. Arinze knew the Igbo names of all the food items they sold in the store, from the crayfish to the oils to the seeds. He could differentiate the egusi from the ogbono. She could not. And, of course, there was the time that Arinze told Mama that he would find himself a good Igbo girl and marry her. He was much younger then, she says, and she laughs a dry, sarcastic laugh. She tells me that perhaps he has changed his mind by now. But even as far back as then, she says, she had no desire to marry a man, much less a Nigerian man she'd never actually met.

'Did you finally get to meet him, then?' I ask.

She nods but doesn't say any more about it. Instead she tells me that she and her mama only stayed a week. They helped to prepare the food for the wedding, pots of egusi soup, okra soup, jolloff rice, fried fish and of course, the ishi ewu delicacy – fried goat head in pepper soup.

They helped to fit Ogechukwu's outfits, too, pinning the sides of the wrappers and the white wedding gown, picking out the beads of her necklaces and the beads of her jigida – her waist beads – which were numerous, about fifteen sets all together, all of different colours. They measured the jigida, fitted them, because she would wear them as she danced, and they would jingle, and onto them money would be stuck. But if they were not correctly fitted, the jigida would start to descend down Ogechukwu's buttocks, down her thighs, with all the dancing that she would do that day, and all the money would drop with them.

'Sounds very festive,' I say, when she finishes. 'Very rich in tradition.'

She nods. 'You should come to mine,' she says.

'Will it make you happy?' I ask.

'Happiness is like water,' she says. 'We're always trying to grab onto it, but it's always slipping between our fingers.' She looks down at her hands. 'And my fingers are thin,' she says. 'With lots of gaps in between.'

I'm not sure how to respond, but I say the first thing that comes to mind: 'I wouldn't know how to behave, all the rites and rituals. I wouldn't know what to wear.'

'Dress as you do to teach,' she says. 'Only remember that after you've dipped your garri in your soup, you must swallow, not chew.' She laughs. 'That will definitely give you away,' she says.

'As if that's the only thing that will,' I say.

We both laugh.

February comes and February goes, and March and April, all passing by with the snow and the bitter cold. The weather reports call for sun throughout the week of her wedding. That week we meet again during my office hours, but she asks that we meet outside of the office, at the park by the river, under the light and dark shadows of the trees. And I agree.

It is mid-afternoon when I make it to the park. The sun is reflecting itself on the river, causing the water to shimmer, like silver and gold threads on a bed of grey silk. I take in the trees that line the trail, each one several yards away from the one before. I take a seat on a bench near one of these trees. I examine it. Its oblong leaves dangle from frail branches and flutter in the air. I reach out and touch the bark of its trunk, which appears jigsaw-like, akin to craters on the surface of the earth. I am still running my fingers across the surface of the trunk, about to pick at a piece of the bark when I catch sight of Grace. My heart skips a beat.

She walks towards me holding a small red box, about the size of her small King James. But it is not the same shade of red as her King James, and around the box strands of gold ribbons have been tied into a bow. Others dangle freely in spirals. She approaches, with slow steps and long strides. She is wearing a mossy green dress that comes down to her ankles. I notice the way her shoulders seem to sag. It causes me to let sag my own. Her loose braids dangle freely around her shoulders, and I take them in, thinking how pretty and dark and youthful they are. And suddenly I'm aware of my age, and of my slumping posture, of my grey hair, and of the wrinkles around my eyes and mouth. I think how counterintuitive my slumping is, how much more the sagging shoulders must be aging me. I sit up, square my shoulders, tuck the loose strands of my hair behind my ears, and wait for her to come to me. All the while, I'm wondering what's in the box.

She takes a seat by me on the bench, on a diagonal, so that she is facing me. Her hands, with the box, are resting on her lap. She taps the box softly then runs her finger along the side of it, along the surface of the ribbons. I watch her fingers move, slowly, delicately. It is almost hypnotic.

I think of Nwafor caressing those fingers, and there is resentment in me. I start to imagine her wedding, but it is interrupted with thoughts of my divorce, of sitting alone by the fireplace at home, listening over and over to the sound of silence, the crackling of wood, the heavy rustling of the leaves outside my windows. And, really, I think, it was all my fault, if it came down to blame. It was my fault for not being able to devote myself to him, to love him completely, the way a wife should love her husband. But there'd been something missing for me in the marriage, and I'd been lonely all the while. I'd have been lonelier if I'd stayed. Because, as if in rebellion, certain emotions become amplified at the exact moments when you are expected not to feel them at all.

I imagine Grace after her divorce, maybe seated by some fireplace, surrounded by silence, by loneliness, and the image, the lonesomeness of it, makes me feel like crying.

The river is just ahead, and I turn my eyes to look at it. I imagine throwing pebbles into it, imagine the small splashes that the pebbles cause as they cut through the surface of the water.

'What's on your mind?' Grace asks me.

'Nothing,' I say.

I can feel her gaze on me, and I imagine she is taking in my wrinkles and all the age spots on my forehead, all those age spots dispersed around the perimeter of my hairline.

'I'm old,' I tell her, forcing myself to chuckle at the statement. 'See the age spots?'

'Yes,' she says. 'Like petals along the fence of a garden. Youthful, really,' she says. 'Like spring.'

I laugh. 'That's a good one,' I say, and I turn to look at her. She is looking very serious about her comment, looking like she is scrutinizing my forehead and getting lost in my age spots.

I try to change the subject. 'The river makes me think of fishing,' I say. 'It would be nice to go fishing one day,' I tell her.

'I don't know how,' she tells me.

'I could teach you,' I say, even though it's been decades since

I went fishing myself, when I was still back in college, still dating my ex-husband, running through wooded campgrounds with him, hiking through secluded, serene forests, the leaves of the trees forming awnings above us. He taught me to fish, I remember then. I begin to wonder how much of it I can still do, and I wonder if I would really be able to teach her. 'It's not so hard casting lines,' I say, not wanting to give in to doubt. As I say it, I imagine us farther down the river, in a canoe maybe, with paddle boats and catamarans sharing the water with us. 'I bet we could hook all sorts. Walleye, crappies, bullheads, catfish, bass, even bluegills.'

She turns her gaze to face the river. She tells me that she hardly recognizes those fish names. Catfish, she knows. Bluegills, too. The rest are new to her, she says. 'Still, it'd be nice to go fishing with you,' she says.

It's a nice thought, she and I fishing together, me teaching her. I feel the rays of the sun on my shoulders, and I hear the distant quacking of the waterfowls. I look at her, and I think how nice it is just to sit here with her.

She clears her throat. And nothing prepares me for what she says next. 'Have you ever been in love?' she asks.

'In love?' I ask.

'Really in love,' she says, 'the kind where every part of you feels like you could spend forever with the person. And you wish that forever could be more than a lifetime. The kind where you don't see all the things that are wrong with the person, all the negatives that should have prevented you from falling for the person in the first place.'

'With love, you see the flaws,' I tell her.

'Then that's what I mean,' she says. 'Only I wouldn't call them flaws.'

I nod. 'I suppose I was in love with my ex-husband,' I say.

'And since then?' she asks. 'How many years now, and you haven't fallen for anyone else?'

'People come and go,' I say, fading away, gazing off somewhere into the horizon. 'And it's hard to find someone with whom you feel truly compatible.'

'I've fallen in love,' she tells me.

It shocks me, this confession of hers, and it scares me, too, and so I force myself not to look at her. 'You've fallen in love?' I say, like an echo, and still I don't look at her.

'Yes,' she says.

'It's not easy identifying love,' I say.

'It's easy enough for me,' she says. 'Love is seeing someone the way God would see that person,' she tells me. 'Seeing in that person something pure and divinely beautiful, seeing in that person the true image of God.'

'You couldn't possibly know what it's like to see someone from the eyes of God.' As I say it, I look up at her, and I examine her, as if examining will give me some clue as to what she is trying to tell me. And it occurs to me that perhaps she is right. Because when I look at her, I see something all-beautiful in her, something all-perfect, if there ever was such a thing.

She leaves where she is sitting on the bench, moves to crouch down in front of me, facing me. She is still holding her little box. She stoops on one knee and looks me in the eye and tells me how it's all wrong. She tells me that, beyond the fact that the Bible condemns that sort of love, she is almost certain that she'll not be good enough, that she couldn't possibly have experienced enough of the world to make it work, to rise to the level of the person she's fallen for. But that she's in love, and she's been trying to fight it, but she can't fight it any more.

'You're getting married,' I remind her. And I imagine the wedding, her mama tinkering with the wedding attire, fussing with the wrappers, placing the jigida beads just so. I imagine that I hear her mama's voice in the wedding hall, sharp and imperious, ordering Arinze around, telling him how to place the chairs, that sort of thing. I imagine Nwafor's face, rough with stubble around the chin and cheeks. A man.

I imagine Grace running her fingers across his face, across his stubble, and I try to imagine her enjoying the sensation. I see his arms coming around her waist, I see her forcing her eyes shut, and when the announcement to kiss the bride is made, I imagine a stiff embrace, an awkward and lifeless peck.

I replace Nwafor with myself. I imagine myself kissing her, and I imagine her leaning into me, running her fingers across the wrinkles on my face, through my greying locks of hair. And I feel myself aching. And I feel something like tears moistening my skin.

'You're getting married,' I say again, in a whisper.

'I know,' she says.

We don't say anything for a while, then she speaks, and the words gush out as if she's in a hurry to spill them. 'You're much older, and I'm much younger,' she says. Her voice is low, and there is a bit of a quiver in it. 'One day, you'll begin to stoop, you might have to rely on a cane, and you'll lose your sight, your hearing, and maybe you'll even begin to lose your mind. And I will love you still. I'll love you the whole way through,' she says. 'I know that I will.'

I turn to look at her, because I believe her. And suddenly I'm extending my hand to slap her across her face, because I understand what she's telling me, and I understand that she's giving me permission to feel a way that I'm not sure I want the permission to feel. But her hand catches mine, as if she has read my mind. And she buries herself into me, wraps her arms around me.

'But then,' she whispers, 'who's to say that I won't die first? Who's to say that you won't be the one burying me?'

'Hush,' I tell her, quietly, shaking my head, and I begin to sob.

As I kiss her, I don't think of the practical things, like what this will mean for my job, the scandal it might cause, the shame it might bring. I don't think of how I will explain all this to my daughter, to her husband, how they will explain it to their son. I don't think of all the scandalous affairs that I've witnessed in my twenty years at the university. I don't think of my reaction to them, not that I've ever been one to condemn, but I don't think of my former disbelief at people – colleagues who, at such distinguished positions at the university, allowed fleeting romances between themselves and their students to interfere with their careers. I don't think of any of this as we kiss.

And I don't think of the Bible, of its verses about unnatural affections and abominations. Because it doesn't feel sinful to me. Because, unlike with Pharaoh and his magicians, none of this is meant to be a challenge to God.

Instead I relent in her arms and think of how good it feels – how nice her skin feels on mine. And I continue to taste her lips, plump and sweet. And I breathe in her scent, flowery and light, something like lavender.

She pulls just a bit away then, fusses with the gold ribbons on the red box, tugs the ribbons until they come undone. She reaches inside the box and takes out a small round object in gold wrapping. She holds out the object in the space above my thighs. 'For you,' she says to me. 'A wedding favour,' she says.

I reach out to accept. She places the object into my cupped hand, and then she covers my hand with her own. Our hands linger in mid-air that way, mine in hers. Then I pull away, because the whole thing feels not quite like a celebration, something like unadorned acceptance, just a bit short of joyful.

And I think that perhaps all this will do. The waterfowls are still quacking, and the sun is high in the sky. The river is still glowing in shades of silver and gold. Grace is sitting next to me, and I can't help thinking that perhaps the verge of joy is its own form of happiness.

Designs

The peeling linoleum on the countertop, near the sink, is the only sign that Celeste was here, that she is gone. It is speckled grey and turned up at one corner like the flap of an old envelope. Celeste's blood, that tiny drip of it, now dry and jagged around the edges, is the envelope's seal; but it is a seal that does nothing to tack the envelope closed.

Ifeinwa stands at the sink, rinsing leaves. She rinses them one by one, and then the tomatoes, and then the carrots. All of them, she rinses carefully, as she would in Port Harcourt; and of course, there, where vegetables are sold fresh from the farm with specks of dirt and sand on them – there, such fervent rinsing would be necessary.

But she is here. Still, she rinses them that old way, as if they have not already been washed and dried and packaged for her to use: it is always some time before the salad is made.

I stand by the door that separates the kitchen from the dining room, and I watch. She is humming, and the sound is like an old lady's song, a folk song, the kind my mama used to sing back home, her legs braced against the sides of the mortar, her arms rising and falling with each strike of the pestle on the yam.

I imagine Ifeinwa back in Nigeria, her wrapper tied around her chest or in a knot above her shoulder. She is in her family's compound, and she is carrying a large bowl on her lap – rinsing palm kernels for oil. Soon, she switches from the kernels to rinsing beans. And after the beans, she pours a small bag of rice onto a tray. She stays with the rice for some time, first shuffling the grains with her fingers, picking out tiny stones as she goes. Then she flips the rice in the tray. With every flip she fills her mouth with air and blows the air over the rice. The chaff rises from the tray like dust in the air. She flips and flips, and she blows air over the rice until chaff no longer rises from it.

I shake the images away. Here, where fruit and vegetables and grains are sold as ready-to-eat, where they glisten under the grocery-store lights, all that cleaning and rinsing is not necessary. I walk over to Ifeinwa at the sink. 'Let me help,' I say. I'm carrying with me two small tubers of yam, purchased on my way back from work, at the African store down the block from Beacon Street.

'You do the yam,' I say, handing the tubers to her. 'I'll finish the salad.'

She laughs. 'I'm taking too long?' she asks. Her voice is soft, and suddenly I'm aware of how smooth her words have become. Already there is that fluidity of American English in her tone, a lilt which took me the better part of a decade to master. Already, she is mastering it.

She lifts her hands from the bowl where the leaves soak. She shakes the water off her hands and dries them on the skirt of her dress. It is autumn, and the window in front of the sink is cracked open. I feel a draught of the cold breeze on my face, and it surprises me that Ifeinwa is even wearing that dress.

'You're not cold?' I ask, eyeing the little red dress. It was I who chose it, who bought it for her, eager for her to fit in. The first time she wore it, she complained of the cold. She changed back into her wrapper and blouse, both of them with the traditional ankara design. I was petulant about the change, but she insisted. They were better, she said, because she could layer the wrapper all around her body, and its warmth would be only a little short of a blanket's.

I continue to eye the dress. 'You're *really* not cold?' I say. I watch as she shakes her head in response. It is not too fervent a shake, but her braids are long, and the movement of her head causes them to whip mildly around her face. I think of Celeste, who does not wear braids, and whose hair is nothing like Ifeinwa's hair.

Ifeinwa speaks, but with my mind on Celeste, the words that reach me are indecipherable, so I have to ask, 'What?'

'Maybe I am, just a little,' she says. She laughs softly. 'You know. A little cold. Maybe I'm just a little cold.'

I nod. 'Yes, of course,' I say, and then I watch her as she moves away from the sink.

She places the yams on the countertop and then picks up the knife. I think of Celeste holding that knife, of Celeste helping me to plant the surprise. I urge myself to stop looking at Ifeinwa, but it is a struggle to stop, and so I watch from the corner of my eye.

Ifeinwa picks up the first tuber of yam. She peels off the bark until all that remains is the flesh, which glows a milky white. She cuts the yam into cubes, the way we do before boiling. Then she reaches up, opens the cupboard, which is not too far above her head. She grabs a pot from there, transfers the cubes into the pot. She moves on to the remaining tuber of yam.

By then I have progressed from the leaves to the carrots and now to the tomatoes. I slice the tomatoes into thin circles, and I watch as Ifeinwa begins to peel the second tuber of yam.

There is a line that runs along the circumference of that yam. Perhaps she doesn't think much of it. I imagine now that if she were to have given it only a bit of thought, she might have commented on how eccentric the yam was, as if it had been cut in half and then stuck back together with a kind of invisible glue. Instead, she proceeds to cut it along that pre-existing line. Suddenly it's as if her knife hits a block. She makes a soft, muffled sound, a bit like a whine. I stop with the toma-toes, and I ask her if something is wrong. But I do not offer to help as I usually do, when, for example, she has trouble opening a jar.

She does it all on her own, carving slowly around the core of the block. There is a look of determination on her face. She digs, fusses, groans. When she arrives at the box, she stays a moment just staring at it. Then she extracts it slowly, cautiously, knowingly. It is a light shade of green, the box, delicate like jade.

She exhales. The sound of her exhale is a little like vindi-cation.

She smiles brightly. The ring inside is just a band. Celeste saw that it was so. Still, Ifeinwa tells me, her eyes glazed with tears, how perfect it is.

I go closer to her. I get down on one knee and I take her starchy hands in mine.

'M huru gin a anya,' she says, looking down at me. Her voice is suddenly heavy with the cadence of Igbo, but it is soft still. I see you in the eyes, she says.

I look up at her – at her teary eyes, her smile, at the braids that dangle limply around her face. 'I love you, too,' I say. And it is true.

That evening, we eat the salad, and then we eat the yam, dipping cubes of it into palm oil – the good old-fashioned way, which is the only way that Ifeinwa will have her yam. This – the yam with palm oil – has become her favourite meal. (She used to buy fufu at the African store down the street. Then she'd spend hours preparing okra soup to eat with the fufu – this used to be her favourite meal. But the odours of the soup and the fufu would rise in the air and would linger, sometimes for days at a time. Eventually I had no choice but to protest. Too rancid, I explained. Not at all American scents.

When she could no longer bear my complaints, she gave in and did away with the fufu and okra soup. She settled for the yam with palm oil.)

After we have eaten, and after Ifeinwa has washed the dishes and I have wiped them dry, she punches the numbers into the phone, all fourteen of them. The phone hangs on the kitchen wall near the fridge and Ifeinwa plays with the dangling cord while she waits for her mother to pick up: she tangles and untangles the cord around her fingers. She does this every time.

'Mama!' I hear her say from where I am sitting in the living room. First her back is to the wall, and she is standing. I am not there with her, but I know that this is so, because this is the way that all her calls go.

Next, there is the sound of her sliding, and I know that she has slipped down to the floor, that she is squatting there, talking to her mama on the phone that way. It is the only way she has done it since she arrived.

'Kedu?' she says. I imagine her mother answering, 'Odi mma.' All is well. I don't listen to what follows next. But I imagine that when she tells her mama the news, her mama screams and asks, 'Ezi okwu?' Is it true? And there is more screaming, happy screaming, and the wrinkles on her mama's face deepen. At least, I imagine they do.

Next comes the talk of when the wedding will be, because, after all, it has now been made official, even more official than my buying the ticket that brought Ifeinwa here. More official than our living together in America for this entire year. I imagine that her mama exclaims again, from the shock of the announcement, as if the proposal is a surprise. She exclaims, as if she didn't see it coming, as if she hasn't always expected it, even from the time I wore maroon knickers and Ifeinwa wore maroon pinafores, from that time when we were mere children in our primary school in Port Harcourt.

We were small children then, and all of us played together, the boys and girls. But we were closer than the rest, Ifeinwa and I, and once, her mama caught me buckling her shoes. It was the harmattan, and there was a breeze, and someone said (her mama or mine), 'Those two will grow up to marry each other some day.' The statement came off sing-songy, light and happy, like a blessing. And after that, it was just assumed that that was the way things would be.

In the living room, I lean my back into the couch. I stretch out my legs in front of me, on the coffee table just ahead. I open the newspaper and wait for Ifeinwa to finish on the phone. My gaze shifts from the newspaper to the window. The curtains are drawn just a little open, like a slit. I look through the slit. Outside, the sky is dark.

Ifeinwa enters the room, beaming. Her smile reminds me of Celeste's, but nothing else about her is like Celeste. She is gentle where Celeste is harsh, submissive where Celeste commands. She was that way even in primary school: pliant and yielding; and so I kept her close.

She waves her fingers in front of me. I fold away the newspaper and smile back, following her with my eyes.

She curls up next to me on the couch. She folds her legs beneath her body and leans her head on my shoulder.

She says, 'So, this is what you and Celeste were doing, all this time? Finding a way to plant my ring into that tuber of yam?'

I smile and nod. 'This is what we've been doing. It pleases you?'

She nods. 'Very much,' she says. 'It pleases Mama too.'

'Good,' I respond. 'Very good.' I pick my newspaper back up, begin to unfold it.

'It's Friday,' she says. 'We have no weekend plans. Nonso, we should celebrate our engagement this weekend.'

I shake my head. 'We should rest,' I say. 'Work has tired me out. We should rest.'

From the corner of my eye, I see that she is nodding slowly – hesitantly nodding her consent. 'Okay,' she says, reluctantly. 'Okay.'

We stay silent for some time, and then she begins again to speak, mumbling something about how maybe I am right about rest, about how her practicum has also tired her out.

A minute goes by, maybe two. Then, 'Actually,' I say, 'maybe we can have a small celebration right now.'

Ifeinwa's eyes light up. She returns to beaming. 'Really?' she asks. It is the tone of hope mixed with surprise, but more than that, it is the tone of gratitude.

I nod with pity at her. 'Yes. *Really*,' I say. I tell her that Celeste will be stopping by soon to drop off some designs. We can celebrate as soon as she arrives, just the three of us.

Her smile fades away, and her eyes grow pensive. And then she says, 'It's late. Past nine o'clock. Celeste will be stopping by again this late?'

'Just to drop off plans,' I say. 'Not to worry. We won't be doing any work tonight. She's just dropping off plans. And then maybe we can celebrate this engagement of ours.'

She rises. I watch as she sets three wine glasses on the table, and I watch as she takes a bottle of wine out of the rack.

There is a painting of us on the wall by the wine rack. It was done the month after she arrived. Those were the days before she enrolled as a nursing student, before she began taking any classes at all.

We were walking along the Charles River, and there was that series of street vendors, who sat on cloths spread across the concrete, and on the grass. There were the graphic artists too, who sat spraying canisters of paint onto large canvases.

Ifeinwa pulled me to one of the graphic artists. We had no pictures of the two of us as adults, she said. And what good were the childhood pictures now? This would be better than any photograph, she said. And so we sat and allowed the vendor to spray his paint, all colours, into portraits in the images of us. She carried the canvas home.

She has just retrieved the corkscrew from the cupboard when we hear the knock on our door. I rise from the couch, and I open the door. Celeste enters, her smile wide, her eyes glowing. Her lashes are long and straight, not tightly curled like Ifeinwa's. She breathes deeply, and I watch its effect on her chest. I step aside and allow her to come in.

Celeste goes straight to Ifeinwa in the dining room. A black leather handbag hangs down from her shoulder. In the opposite hand she carries a grey plastic tube, the designs rolled up inside. She holds on to her bag but sets the tube on the table. The cylinder rolls back and forth, just a little, before it finally settles to a stop.

Celeste takes Ifeinwa's hand in hers. They mock-examine the ring. They laugh and they hop about like little girls in a playground, primary-school students who have been let outside for recess after lunch.

I am standing under the archway between the living room and the dining room. I observe them from there.

Ifeinwa sees me where I am standing and calls me to join them. I walk a few steps into the dining area, a few steps to one of the chairs that surround the table. Ifeinwa fills the glasses with the wine before I have taken my seat on the chair.

When we have all three taken our seats, Celeste raises her glass high and calls for a toast. I raise my glass as well, and Ifeinwa joins.

'A long and happy marriage,' Celeste says. It is a brief toast. Just that. But it appears to have all the power of those long, extended toasts: Ifeinwa smiles demurely and thanks Celeste in a wholehearted sort of way.

All the while Celeste, seated by my side, has already begun allowing her gaze to linger on me.

Celeste and I first met at the university, the month I arrived. We met the very first day of classes. Just a simple hello. It was August, and in Nigeria the sun would have been strong as well; and if it rained, there would have been that same scent of wet concrete.

But in Nigeria there would have been other things too: the scent of crushed millipedes. That sandy scent of snails.

I loved August in America the same way that I loved it in Nigeria, the same way that I loved the rain, and the scent of millipedes, and the scent of snails. I loved August with the same intensity with which I would eventually despise the autumn, and especially the winter – that cold, dark season that brought me to the brink of despair.

But then, there was the matter of Celeste. *She* was the reason that I began to love the cold: Celeste with her wide smile and pencilled-in brows. Celeste with her brassy hair. She should have been a brunette, but she had grown accustomed to dyeing. She dyed even during those early days of graduate school. Sometimes she waited too long to dye, and her natural colour crept in and threatened to blossom, like weeds on grass.

She was the reason, with her long, manicured nails, with red lipstick that made her lips shine like plastic. Buxom Celeste whose full chest appeared to do battle with the seams of her blouses. 'They're real,' she'd say, back then. As if she could read my mind.

When the autumn came that first year, it was she who offered to show me a place where I could buy a coat. She did not take me to any of those little boutique stores around the university. She knew that I could not afford those.

We got on the tram, took seats by the window. I looked outside for most of the ride, afraid to speak, afraid of all the ways in which my accent could betray me.

But Celeste asked questions that forced me to speak. 'What is Port Harcourt like?' she asked. 'Have you lived anywhere in Nigeria outside of there?' She told me that she had a great uncle and a great aunt who once lived in Nigeria. In Port Harcourt, she said. GRA. Of course, that was way back then, before Independence, she said.

I asked, 'Way back then? During the time that the colonial masters were settling in, building their mansions and their clubhouses and making servants of the Nigerians?' They were English, but they brought with them some Americans too, I said.

I imagined GRA then, what it must have looked like during the reign of the colonial masters – devoid of rubbish heaps, a network of paved roads, estates of majestic houses with cylindrical columns marking their fronts. Houses like government buildings, with pipe-borne water and the kind of serenity that plenty of money brings. I told Celeste all this.

When I was done, Celeste shook her head slowly. 'Sorry,' she said, her first apology. And it was sincere.

She took me to the Salvation Army on Mass Ave. She searched through the racks with me. She used on the coats the same soothing voice she would later use on me, the kind Mama used to use on the chickens in our back yard. They'd run freely around the compound, but every once in a while, she'd choose one for stew. She'd chase it around, making those soft, cooing sounds. The chicken waddled away but eventually Mama won.

At the Salvation Army, the coats on the rack brushed against Celeste's hands, the fabrics sliding between and around her fingers like vines crawling all over a gate.

When she found the coat, she shook it as if to air it out. She continued to shake, to get a better sense of the coat. Its sleeves writhed all around her, from the force of the shake.

She handed it over to me when she was done. A prickly heat appeared to have radiated up her face by then, rendering her cheeks red. All that fervent shaking. I observed the heat on her face, and I seemed to absorb it from her: first, I felt it in the soles of my feet, and then it crept up to my thighs. It was the strongest in my groin, and then in my chest. From my chest, it radiated up to my face.

It was then that I understood. That there was something else to it.

Ifeinwa toys with the ring around her finger, turning it clockwise and then counter-clockwise. Celeste sips from her glass of wine. I watch them both.

'The next step is deciding a date,' Celeste says.

Ifeinwa nods. 'It might be far, the date,' she says. 'You see, the traditional wedding will have to be done in Nigeria. Planning for all that will take some time.'

Celeste turns to me. 'I imagine it's a lot to plan,' she says.

I nod.

She begins to rise from her seat. 'Well,' she says. 'It's certainly getting late. Thank you for the wine. But time for me to head back home.'

Ifeinwa rises and walks Celeste to the door. I rise too.

At the door, they hug. I stand behind Ifeinwa, and when they are done with their hug, my hands find their way to Ifeinwa's waist. They rest there, lightly, in the groove between her waist and her hips. Celeste looks in the direction of my hands. She doesn't move to hug me too. Instead she raises a hand and waves.

It is some time, five or so minutes, before I open the tube of designs. I slide the designs out, and I announce to Ifeinwa that I should have returned the tube right away to Celeste. I tell her that I will run downstairs with it. Who knows, perhaps I will catch Celeste still on Lenox Street, maybe at worst on Beacon Street.

Ifeinwa only nods. For a moment I think I see a question forming in her eyes. But she shakes it away. 'Well, hurry up,' she says.

Just outside our building, there is a courtyard. The courtyard is all concrete, save for the swings and slides and see-saws, which are plastic and metal and nearly colourless in the dark.

We are standing beyond where the courtyard is, at a distance from the entrance of the building. We are one level above the courtyard, at the top of the steps that lead to the street. We stand there, because there is where Celeste has chosen to wait for me.

I lean on the black metal railing near the top of the steps. It is a little to the corner, not directly visible from the steps.

Celeste leans against me. A cedar tree hovers above us. Its aroma is spicy but also like the scent of berries and nuts: it mixes well with the lavender of Celeste's body.

There is a little light coming from a street lamp not far away, which causes there to be shadows. Our shadows on the grey concrete walkway are long.

Celeste leans harder against me so that I can feel the pressure of the railing on my bottom and on the backs of my upper thighs. She buries her face in the crook of my neck. She kisses me there. They are light – barely there, the kisses – like the brush of a butterfly's wings.

'Lucky man that you are,' she says. 'Having your cake and eating it too.' The words come out muffled, but I feel her lips on the skin of my neck. I feel them mouthing the words.

I rub my chin. My fingernails rake through my beard. The sound is something like discord, like the rustling of leaves, only louder. 'It's not ideal,' I say.

Celeste says, 'What she doesn't know can't hurt her.'

I stay silent for some time. Then, 'No,' I say. 'What she doesn't know certainly cannot hurt her. Besides, a man's got to do what a man's got to do.'

She chuckles softly. She kisses me on the lips and lingers. She teases and bites and lingers some more. She tugs at my waistband and pulls out the hem of my tucked shirt. She runs her fingers under the shirt. She moans. Beneath our feet the cones of the cedar crumble.

It is probably after midnight by then. There are no children's voices emerging from the courtyard, no adult chatter, no laughter. Just the sound of a cone or two falling to the ground, the sound of Celeste and me crumbling them under our shoes.

There are the rustling of perhaps a pair of squirrels, their tiny feet cutting across the concrete and the grass. The crickets chirp, those mating sounds that are a little like sounds of alarm.

My hands move against Celeste's body wilfully, as they have done all these years, all the mornings and afternoons at the firm, or in the apartment, while Ifeinwa is away at class.

I slide her skirt upwards, so that it bunches at the fullest part of her hips. I place my legs between her legs, force her thighs open that way.

She is tugging at the front of my trousers, at the zipper there, when the shadow emerges from the direction of the courtyard, from the direction of the steps. I look up to take it in completely with my eyes. When I do, I see that Ifeinwa is the shadow, that she has stopped in her tracks, and that she is watching me. She holds her arms around her body, because, of course, in that dress, she is cold.

Even in the near darkness, there is something pure about her face. It is after all artless and unprocessed in a way that Celeste's is not.

Ifeinwa's face isn't angry, only more than a little bewildered. She jerks her head around as if she doesn't know where to look.

I allow Celeste to continue with my zipper. I pull her skirt further up. I lift her until her feet no longer touch the ground. I raise myself from the railing so that I'm no longer leaning on it.

Celeste raises her legs, wraps them tightly around me so that they take up the space between the railing and my back.

I kiss Celeste forcefully, defiantly. I unbutton her blouse so that her brassiere shows from the front. I am astonished by my cruelty, so I pretend that Ifeinwa is not really there.

'Nonso!' Ifeinwa screams. She steps forward, continues towards me. Celeste tenses up. All movements cease.

I loosen my grip on Celeste. I lower her so that her feet return to the ground. She pulls her skirt back down over her hips, her thighs. She does not bother to cover her bare chest. She turns so that she is facing Ifeinwa.

'Chi m o!' Ifeinwa exclaims. 'My God!' Then, 'Nonso, what are you doing? What have you done?' She glares at me, then she turns her head, her eyes so that she is no longer looking at me, so that she is looking directly into Celeste's face.

'Sorry,' says Celeste. It comes out forcefully and soft at once. It is the second time that I see her apologize. It is not sincere. She says the word, but her eyes are cold and impenitent, as if she is resenting the fact that she should have to apologize at all.

My eyes shift from Celeste to Ifeinwa. For a short while, I take turns between the two of them, glancing erratically from one to the other. Finally my eyes settle again on Celeste. I observe the look of self-satisfaction, now even a little more like triumph, on her face. The realization is something like the movement of air, slow-forming, impalpable at first, then building and building until it is quite visible to my eyes, until the branches shake and quiver in the wind, until the leaves hop and skip about. I scowl, because it is only then that I realize my servant role in all of this.

That same scent of lavender is emanating from her but suddenly it appears acrid, like the odour of fufu, except worse. It is terrible, the stench, the most offensive one that I've breathed in all of my life.

Still, I breathe. A deep, resounding breath, before a painful silence.

Tumours and Butterflies

This past summer, Papa finds out that it's thyroid cancer, and Mama calls me on the phone to tell me what it will mean. 'First he'll need surgery,' she says. 'And then, very likely, radiation. I'll need all the help I can get,' she adds, and I can tell that she is serious: her accent is heavy – English, but with the cadence and intonation of Igbo – the way it often is when she has something important to say. 'Your papa,' she says, 'don't worry about him. He's a sick man now. Besides, he knows better.'

We go back and forth. I tell her she's wrong. I'm sure he doesn't know any better. She tells me that cancer is no joke, that it's like looking death straight in the eyes.

'Believe me,' she says, 'I know what things have been like in the past. But this time is different. He knows better for sure.'

I'm sitting on the floor of my apartment, drawing circles with my fingers on the beige carpet, leaning my head on the seat of my sofa. There is a pile of papers – essays – by my side. I should be grading them, filling their margins with marks, inserting carets, striking through words. Instead I'm listening to Mama's voice on the phone, drawing circles on the carpet and staring out my open balcony door.

Outside, the sky is greying, and the sun looks like a fuzzy, deep-orange ball in the clouds. I look down at the carpet with the circles that I've drawn. There is a dark spot in the middle of one of the loops, and for whatever reason, maybe because I am talking with her on the phone, or maybe because we're talking about Papa, I see her face in that area of the carpet, and

I see the dark spot above her left cheekbone. It reminds me of the picture on her Massachusetts driver's licence, in which she's sporting the remains of a black eye.

When I think of Massachusetts, I think of overfed cockroaches and mice, inflated and brown, brazen and indiscreet, not like the ones in Port Harcourt. They were the first things we met in our apartment on Comm Ave. Even now in my apartment in Pennsylvania, three or so hundred miles away, sometimes I can almost hear the scurrying of the mice, the sounds that their little feet made as they scampered about the tattered linoleum of that tired, old kitchen in Boston.

When I think of Massachusetts, I think also of that cold and windy November day, the day we came, Mama and I, in our matching cotton dresses, Papa in his finest isiagu, patterned with gold lion heads embroidered on the main fabric.

Even the heavier fabric of the isiagu did not do much to protect him from the cold. It did only a little more than the cotton of our dresses did for us.

But mostly, when I think of Massachusetts, I remember the period when Mama went on that trip to Florida, just a few months after we arrived.

Someone, another international student in Papa's engineering programme, tells Papa and Mama about a church group that's offering to help us get working papers and possibly even help us become legal permanent residents. During the day, Papa attends classes at Boston University. During the nights, he works as the superintendent of the building where we live. In exchange for free housing in the basement apartment and some pocket change, he sweeps floors and takes out trash from the lounges. He answers the calls of the residents. If they are locked out of their apartments, he opens the doors. If a light bulb is broken, he replaces it. It is a 24/7 job, and combined with his classes, he has no choice but to stay back. Mama heads off to Florida on her own.

Those days, we get our food from the food bank at the church on Beacon Street. Mama makes sure to get the supplies before she leaves. Two boxes of cornflakes, a box of cherry-flavoured Fruit Roll-Ups, a loaf of bread, tomatoes, onions and a bag of rice. From Christie's Market, she buys some oranges and bananas, and a carton of milk, because there are no oranges or bananas or milk at the food bank. She buys a crate of eggs, because the eggs at the bank are always several weeks expired. I am seven, almost eight years old, and the day Mama leaves for Florida, she wakes me up early to say goodbye. 'Be good,' she says. 'Take care of your father.' I nod, though I'm not sure what that will mean.

That evening, Papa returns from school or work, I don't know which.

'Papa, welcome,' I say, like I always do, when he enters the apartment. I am in the kitchen, rummaging in the fridge for something to eat.

'You're hungry?' he asks. His voice is serious.

I close the fridge and look at him. I nod.

'Okay,' he says. 'Okay.' He puts down the bag that is hanging from his shoulder, runs his hand back and forth over his head. 'You can go watch television in the living room. I'll get something ready for us.'

From the living room, I hear metal clanging on metal. I hear whisking in a bowl. When Papa calls me to eat, there is a small tray of toasted bread, a stick of butter on a white saucer, and a plate of something in between scrambled eggs and an omelette, tomato and onion cubes scattered evenly, jagged and protruding, like raised scars across the top.

We eat together that evening, and even if the omelette is runny and bland, and even if the toast is charred on one side, I eat them all as if I'm eating one of Mama's dishes – her rice and beans or her beef stew or her okra soup. I lick my lips and tell him thank you when I'm done. I clear the table, and he helps me. I tuck that evening away in my memory, safely, so that I do not forget it, because I am seven, almost eight years old, and it is the first time that I am seeing this side of him.

A couple of days later, Mama returns from Florida. She doesn't get the working papers. It even turns out that the church organization might be a scam. I'm sitting in my room when I hear her tell this to Papa. He grunts and tells her to hush. How would she know a scam from real, he asks. She says she knows. He tells her to hush again. 'This is what happens when you send a woman to take care of business,' he says. 'An utter disaster,' he says.

I come out of my room when he has gone into theirs. Her luggage is on the living-room floor. She smiles at me when she sees me, pats me on the shoulder, asks me if I'm hungry. 'Yes,' I say. 'Very hungry,' and it's the truth. It is late evening by then, and, knowing that Mama would be returning that day, Papa did not prepare anything for dinner.

Mama nods and tells me she'll go get some groceries straight away, from the African store off Beacon Street, not too far from where we live. Today is a celebration that calls for Nigerian food, she says, because for now it seems we have no choice but to remain Nigerians. 'Might as well make it a cele-bration,' she says. 'No need to lament who we are.' I watch her walk towards the door, and I make a motion to follow, even if I don't have my shoes on. 'Stay,' she says. 'I'll be back before long.' I lean on the door and watch her walk away. My stomach is growling, but all I can do is watch. When she turns the corner – when I can't see her any more – I shut the door and fasten the latch.

She comes back before long, like she says. She cooks up the meal, whistling and humming the whole time. Then she dishes out some of the food for Papa, a tray of egusi soup, which she makes from the fresh egusi seeds that she gets from the Nigerian store. On the tray there is also a round ball of garri. She takes the tray to Papa in his room, still whistling and smiling and bopping her head just a bit, even as she enters the room. It is silent for a while and then I hear his voice. I don't hear her voice, and meanwhile I'm thinking how I wish she'd hurry up in there, because hunger is about to kill me. Then something in me suddenly becomes afraid. I go to my room and wait. His voice grows louder, scolding, and there is a loud smacking sound. And still she does not come out. And still, his scolding voice.

At first I want to run out to her, but I am too afraid. But then even the fear becomes too much to bear, and so I come out of my room again, make my way to the kitchen, inch closer and closer to their bedroom. On the wall dividing their bedroom from the living room is a black shelf. I am hiding to the side of the shelf, crouched down on my knees, when I see Mama come out of the room with the tray. She goes back into the kitchen, shaking her head from side to side. She fusses with the pots and pans and then she heads back to his room with another tray of food.

A little later that evening, the area around her left eye starts to grow darker. Mostly, this is what I remember when I think of Massachusetts.

The next few days, I can't stop thinking of Mama's voice on the phone, telling me she needs all the help she can get. I can't walk down the hallways of Allen High School, I can't eat dinner, without hearing her voice, pleading for me to come home. A week later, I make the decision.

School has not yet let out for the summer, so I take an emergency leave of absence, and a substitute teacher takes over for me.

They don't live in Boston any more. They are now in New Jersey, because Papa found himself a better-paying job there with Bristol-Myers Squibb. Before that he worked for several different pharmaceutical companies, the first of which was the reason we were able to remain in the States. That first one had been willing to sponsor him for permanent residency, which made it so that we could legally stay.

In any case, prior to his falling sick, he worked for the manufacturing engineering sector of Bristol-Myers. Mama said he helped to produce medications to treat everything from arthritis to cardiovascular disease, from cancer to psychiatric disorders. As I pack my bags, I find myself wondering if he manufactured the medications that will be used to treat him now.

They live a couple of hours' drive from me, US-22E to PA-33S all the way to I-287S and then to Route 1. When I finally arrive, I park my car in front of the house, and I breathe. It is the first time in years, about ten years now, that I am allowed to come home.

She has left the key for me underneath the doormat. When I bend down to retrieve it, I recognize the doormat, the same one from nearly a decade ago. But it's still looking brand new, not fraying at the edges at all. I wonder how often doormats are replaced. I wonder if they have just gotten into the habit of replacing it with the exact same type. I wonder if maybe there is just no-one stepping on the mat, perhaps it is always just the two of them, never any guests, never any extra footsteps.

The house is a bi-level. I climb up the staircase. The living room is at the top of the staircase, to the left. To the left of that is the doorway to their bedroom. The door is pulled closed, and though I know that he's not in there, that he is in some room in Saint Peter's Hospital, probably wearing one of those pale blue gowns whose open back is only drawn together by a pair of thin strings, though I know that he is quite a distance away, prepping for thyroid surgery, I feel the muscles of my stomach tighten.

I head for my old room. I turn the knob and stare for a bit. On my old dresser are two rows of stuffed animals: purple baby Dumbo with his large, drooping ears; yellow ducks in a line, some ripped at the seams, others with deep red, almost brown blotches – dried blood – marking their bodies: old consequences of Papa's rage; little Sacagawea with her long braids and her peeling, dangling eyelashes. I shake the dust off them. I watch the dust particles scatter in the air. Then I run my hand across the back of one of the ducks and pick it up. It's been years since I picked any of them up, years since I talked to them, hushed, in the dark, staining them with tears, telling them my list of things I'd take with me when I turned eighteen and left. When I put the duck back down, back with the group, I imagine that they begin again to talk amongst themselves, like we used to when I was one of them. Only, now I am a stranger. I don't talk to them, and I barely listen.

The bed is made with pale yellow sheets that I do not recognize, but my old comforter is folded at the foot, as if it has been waiting there these ten years, anticipating my return.

I sit on the bed, close my eyes for a moment. I breathe in, inhale the musty, stale air, and then I open up my eyes and look in the direction of the window. The curtains are pulled open, and the sunlight enters. I can see its rays, a light-yellowish diagonal line from the windows down to the floor, with dust particles like minuscule butterflies floating in it. On the area of the carpet where the light lands, the curtain's embroidered leaves appear to float too, drifting shadows on the rug. I stare at the drifting leaves, allow myself to be hypnotized by them, but it's a melancholic sort of hypnosis, the kind where you find yourself reliving all the things you wish you never had to live at all.

They had an argument my senior year in high school. One of the serious ones. I got in the middle of it, screamed, told him what a horrible father he was. Pushed him away from her. What kind of husband beats his wife? I asked.

Suddenly his hand was coming down hard on my face, his tight fist landing right smack on my mouth.

We still don't know who called the police, and we certainly did not hear them knock, if at all they knocked. One moment, Papa's hand is coming down on my face, the next moment a couple of officers in dark uniforms with guns and badges are appearing in the doorway of Mama and Papa's bedroom, which is where we were at the time.

So, the officers arrive, and for a time both of them stay with us in the house, asking questions, taking notes. Then one of them tells Mama and me to follow him. He leads us outside.

I sit on the hood of Papa's Ford Taurus. The tears dry on my face, and the skin on my cheeks feels stiff, as if all the moisture in it has dried away with the tears. There is a cool breeze, and I turn my face into it and right into the scrutinizing gaze of the officer.

'Your lips are bleeding,' the officer says, staring at me. 'You'll have to tell me who did it to you.'

I touch my lips. The blood is caked, congealed by the air. It feels bumpy like a scab.

'You'll have to tell me who did it to you,' the officer says again.

From the corner of my eye, I see Mama blinking purposefully and shaking her head at me. 'What will happen if I tell you?' I ask the officer, picking at the congealed blood, wiping it away with the sleeve of my shirt.

'It's a crime,' the officer says. 'The person responsible will be arrested and put in jail.'

Mama blinks some more.

'Don't worry,' the officer says. 'A little jail time will teach him a lesson. He'll know better than to do it again.'

'Your father is diabetic,' Mama bursts out then. 'Do you want to be the one to send a diabetic man to jail? What will happen to him there? Do you want to be responsible for destroying his health?'

'Ma'am,' the officer says.

'I fell,' I say. 'It's my fault. I fell on my face.'

The officer stares at me hard, jots down some notes. Before long he and his partner are inside their police cruiser, backing out of the driveway.

The next day, period four, Mrs Beatty's calculus class, the intercom goes off, and I hear my name. 'Uchenna Okoli, please report to Mr Loftin's office.'

Mr Loftin is the guidance counsellor, and in his office, he pulls out the local newspaper, turns to the last few pages of it, asks me if everything is okay at home.

I tell him yes.

He looks at me as if he is inspecting me, as if I am an experiment and he's watching to write a report.

He says, 'I don't know any other family by the name of Okoli in the entire of Edison Township. As a matter of fact, I don't know any other Okolis at all.'

I nod. 'It's a rare name,' I say. I try to chuckle, but it comes out like a cough. I put my right arm on the armrest and act like I'm merely relaxing into the chair. Then I lean my head on my hand and cover a good portion of my lips that way.

He nods. 'Your family was cited for an incident of domestic violence,' he says. 'You're the only Okoli family I could find in Edison.'

Tears well up in my eyes, not because I'm sad or embarrassed. Tears well up because suddenly I feel relieved.

'Do you want to talk about it?' Mr Loftin asks.

I nod and start to speak. 'My father,' I say. I pause.

'Your father?' Mr Loftin asks.

'Yes,' I say. 'He gets angry.'

'Did he do something to you?' Mr Loftin asks.

Do you want to be responsible for sending a diabetic man to jail? I hear in my head.

I wipe my eyes and smile. 'It doesn't matter,' I say. 'Everything will be fine.'

Mr Loftin nods.

I say, 'You know, I have a perfect 4.0. I'm in all those AP classes. I've taken the tests and have a semester worth of AP credits. Before you know it, I'll be in college. And I'll do well in college. Everything will be fine.'

It comes out like a rehearsed speech, which is sort of what it is, because I've told it to myself so many times those past few months, every time Papa lashed out at Mama and me.

Mr Loftin nods. 'You'll do just fine in college, yes,' he says. 'But there are other issues. I can't help you if you don't talk to me.'

I shake my head.

'Are you sure?' he asks.

I nod.

'I'll be here if you change your mind,' he says, as I get up to leave.

Somewhere in the middle of going to and from the hospital, I find out that the thyroid gland is butterfly-shaped, that its two lobes look somewhat like wings. Butterflies should be soft and beautiful, but I imagine that perhaps this is the issue with Papa's thyroid. Perhaps his thyroid has never been quite the way it should be. I imagine that removing it from his neck might result in the change that we've always wanted.

He stays in the hospital for a week. The surgery is simple, goes exactly as expected, the doctors say. He will be back to normal within a couple of days of being discharged, they tell us.

He comes home, walks around in his blue-and-white-striped pyjamas for more than a couple of days. He drags his feet, mutters.

We beg him to eat, but he shakes his head and tells us that he has no appetite. One week passes. Two weeks pass. 'It's a shame,' he says one evening. His voice is throaty and his accent is heavy like Mama's. 'Such a shame to be so sick and weak.'

'Munchausen's syndrome,' I whisper to Mama when we leave him.

She scowls at me.

'Better this way,' I tell her. 'I'll take Munchausen any day over the shouting and the hitting.'

She is wearing her mauve gown. It is sleeveless and goes down to her ankles. Her cheekbones are high, and the skin on her face appears supple and young. At first glance, hers is not the face of a fifty-five-year-old woman. But there are grey bags under her eyes. And her forehead wrinkles just a bit, like the creased linen of her gown. She looks at me and shakes her head. 'Don't call trouble where there's no trouble,' she says.

She is right about there not being trouble. For once, Papa is placid, docile.

That evening, Papa calls my name. He calls it loudly, so that I can hear it even from the kitchen, even with their bedroom door being shut. He is sitting up on his bed when I open the door, his back facing the wall. His comforter is a tawny landscape of purple and green swirls, like little snakes on sandy desert land. It is pulled midway up his torso. I stand at the entrance of the room, just under the arch of the doorway. 'Yes, Papa?' I say.

He is wearing a white singlet and fussing with his comforter. He asks for a glass of water. 'Are you okay?' I ask.

He nods slowly as if his head is a heavy ball on his neck, as if any movement must be slow and calculated in order that the ball does not tip over.

I leave the room to fetch his water. When I return, I walk up to his bedside. I hold the glass of water out to him. 'What a wonderful child,' he says, as he takes the glass from me. 'You're so good to your poor old papa.' His voice is gentle, and the words are kind and unexpected. So unexpected that all I hear is what I've gotten accustomed to hearing from him, especially those last few years at home, my high-school years: I hear in his voice something gravelly and harsh, which causes me to grimace and pucker my brows the way I would at the sound of fingernails scraping across a chalkboard. But then I think of his cancerous butterfly, and I think of tumours extending out of its lobes, out of its wings. I think of the doctors plucking the tumours out, tossing them away. I think of the medications stabilizing him in a way that his diseased thyroid did not manage to do. Only then do I recognize his voice for what it is: a soft and gentle embrace.

★

My second month in college, I called and called Mama on the phone, but she did not pick up. After a week of my calling, she finally called back.

That day, I pick up the phone, and I've barely said hello when she says, 'Now that you have gone off to college, your father does not feel that it is a good idea that you come back. He feels you have been disrespectful to him by interfering with things in our marriage, by getting involved.'

'Me? Disrespectful?' I ask.

'Yes,' she says. 'There've been times when you got in the middle of our fighting,' she says. 'When your parents are having an argument, it's not your place to get involved.'

'It wasn't just an argument,' I say. 'He was hitting you.'

'He says I should tell you that he is disowning you,' she says.

At first, I'm silent. Then I tell her that she is weak. I ask her how she can be so unemotional, how she can even dare to relay the message as if she's just stating a fact. My voice is shaking the whole time, still I force myself to finish: I ask her if she even bothered to tell him that he was the one at fault, that he had no business disowning me? I don't wait for an answer, because I already know the answer. I hang up the phone, because, deep down, I understand that this is what she feels is right, this is what she believes she needs to do.

For Christmas break, I pack up some of my things from the dorm room and stay in my friend Melissa's empty apartment. State College is dead and cold during the winter break, but I decide that there is something to be said for a real, honest winter, that there's something enjoyable about tumbling in and sliding on piles of unmuddied snowflakes. So I put on my boots, take the tray that I had previously stolen from the dining commons outside with me. I lay the tray on the ground. I sit on it, and I slide down the small hills of the snow-covered fields, over and over again. I do this almost every other day. Before long Christmas break is over.

The entire spring semester, I don't hear from her, and then in the summer Mama calls, tells me that we can arrange something, a meeting at the mall, maybe. Perhaps I can even sneak into the house when he has gone to bed. I can park my car two streets down from the house. We can catch up while he sleeps, like good old times, maybe even watch some of the newest Nollywood movies together. *What good old times?* I wonder, but I don't say it to her. Instead I'm thinking of the dozen or so times we watched a movie. Almost every one of those times, Papa came in, took the remote control, and changed the channel to some WWF match or whatever else he claimed he had to watch. The last few times, we'd decided to wait till late, till he was asleep. And we'd watched the movie quietly and stiffly, worried that Papa would somehow come in and change the channel on us.

Still, that summer, I go to her. We meet at the mall, have dinner at the Chinese place. After dinner, she leaves. I wander the mall, read at the Borders bookstore to kill time. At around 10 p.m., I go to the house. We are sure he'll be asleep.

Weeks go by, and then a month. By then, Allen High School has adjourned for summer break. Mama and I continue to take Papa back and forth for his check-ups. Everything seems to be going fine, and I'm thinking that my services are no longer even needed, and then suddenly, one day, Mama and Papa return from the check-up, and he goes directly to his room. He looks to be in a bad mood, so I ask Mama what it's all about. Mama announces to me then that he will indeed need to go in for radiation. She tells me that she will need to prepare low-iodine diets for him, because limiting his intake of iodine

before the radiation treatment will help increase the effective-
ness of the radioactive iodine in his body.

'What does a low-iodine diet mean?' I ask her.

'No seafood,' she says. 'No dairy products, no egg yolks, no
soybeans, no Red Dye #3. Rice, fresh meats and cereals in
moderation. Plenty of unsalted nuts and fresh fruit, except
rhubarb and maraschino cherries (the ones that contain Red
Dye #3).' She says it dutifully, carefully, as if she's memorized
the doctor's pamphlet.

'It's a lot of planning and preparation,' she says. 'And it will
only get worse when the treatment is done.'

I only listen.

'I need more help,' she says. 'You'll have to stay a bit longer.'

I nod, because things haven't been so bad.

'I have to think of my work,' Mama goes on. 'I really can't
afford to lose my job.'

I think about my first year in college, how I was banned
from coming home, how she compromised and allowed me to
sneak in at night. There's something different, something almost
satisfying in being wanted. I nod and tell her that I'll stay a
while longer.

Mama has to work the day he undergoes the radiation treatment. She has used up all her vacation and personal days, and
taking a leave of absence from her job would mean going
without health insurance for that period of time, which is not
an option with Papa still needing treatment.

I drive him to his appointment, and the plan is that he'll
take a taxi back, because there's no telling how long he'll need
to be in the hospital.

After I drop him off, I head to the Borders by the mall. I
find a small cubicle and sit there, reading the newspaper. Then

I switch from the newspaper to a collection of short stories, and before I know it, it's evening. I return the book to the shelf where I found it, and I head home.

By now Mama has made me a copy of the house key, so I open the door and enter. I'm only halfway up the stairs when I see the signs that Papa has posted. Four of them, printed in red ink, on white paper. They all read: CAUTION! RADIATION! STAY AT LEAST THREE FEET AWAY! Even though things for the past month have not been bad at all with Papa, and even though, with the passage of time, I'm getting more and more confident with my diseased butterfly theory, the obligation to stay away causes me to sigh with relief.

I walk between the dining room and the kitchen. There are two long lists, duplicates of post-treatment procedures. The lists begin: for the first two days, maintain a prudent distance from others. Sleep alone in a separate room. Avoid close prolonged social contact as much as possible. Use only separate, disposable eating utensils. Do not prepare food for others or have any prolonged contact with foods of others.

I am still reading the list when my cell phone rings. It is Mama on the line.

'When your father is ready to eat,' she says, 'put some of the yam and spinach pottage onto a plate, heat it up in the microwave for two and a half minutes, then transfer the food onto one of the paper plates from the dining room. Place the food on the small table by your papa's bedroom door. Knock on the door when you've placed it there. He will come out and take the food when he hears the knock.'

'How will I know when he's ready to eat?' I ask. She works at Sayreville Assisted Living Home, at least twenty minutes away. She works the 3 p.m. to 11 p.m. shift. I imagine her in her nurse's station, leaning towards old Jack and his metal walker, her mouth close to his one good ear, coaxing him loudly to give her just one moment, one moment so that she can make this call to me. 'How will I know when?' I ask.

'I'll give him your cell phone number,' Mama says. 'Some time within the next hour, he will send you a text message telling you that he is ready. That way you'll know to prepare the food.' My heart starts to beat fast. I feel like suddenly there is no air going into my lungs, but I know I need to say something. Before I can respond, she says she has to go and hangs up the phone.

I was a senior in college the last time Papa lost his job. Over five years ago, almost six now. Not that he hadn't been laid off from jobs before, but this was the first time that he had trouble getting another job right away. This was also the period when he first began to fall sick. First there was the lump in his neck, then the hoarseness, the problems swallowing, the difficulty breathing. He was in and out of the hospital even then.

One evening during that time, Mama calls me at my dorm room in the university, tells me that she thinks it would be a good idea for me to write to him, to show him some sympathy in this time of distress. 'I make no excuses for the man,' she says. 'Your father has done many things wrong, but he's a sick man now. A sick man without a job.'

I say no. The line seems to go dead. 'Hello?' I say. 'Hello?'

She doesn't say anything, but just as I am about to hang up the phone, she clears her throat and tells me she is disappointed, that she has to go. She hangs up the phone.

Days later, as I'm about to run off to class, the phone rings. It is Mama again, and we have the same conversation once more. 'Be the bigger person; forgive and forget,' she says. 'Write him the letter, or an email even, show him you're the bigger person, that you can be sympathetic, especially to someone like him. Forgive and forget.' That's what she's had to do, she says.

As we get off the phone, I tell her that I'll think about it. And I do.

Nearly a week later, I'm sitting in my dorm again, at my desk area, when I decide to call her back. She picks up, and from the sound of her voice, I can tell that she is expectant.

I ask her if she knows what she is asking me to do. She says yes, she realizes what she is asking. Write the letter, she says. He is a changed man. He is changing as we speak, what with all these bad things happening to him, a man can't help but change for the better.

'How long has this change been going on?' I ask, disbelieving. Just a year before she had called me crying about how he brought the car to a stop, dragged her out by the hair, slammed her onto the body of the car, screaming at her, all because she had made a comment about his speeding. After that incident, she had promised that she would leave, would come and find an apartment near me, anything to get away from him.

I remind her that before that, he kicked her out of the car in the middle of the highway on their way to some church conference, forced her to find her own way home.

I tell her that some things, and some people, don't change. 'It's no different from when we lived in Massachusetts,' I tell her. 'Even then he was banning us from entering his car if he happened to find crumbs or dirt that he thought we had tracked in.' Does she remember how I saved up two hundred dollars from babysitting kids around the block, from collecting and recycling empty cans and bottles from the streets every day after school, just so that I could help her buy her own car? Does she remember how she worked twelve hours a day at her under-the-table housekeeping job at Beacon Hill Hotel, changing sheets and scrubbing toilets, so that we could put together our money, so that we could buy her that Dodge Omni, the maroon one with the peeling paint, which ran just fine, but was sold so cheap because of its terrible paintwork? I was only in middle school then. 'Do you remember?' I ask.

'I remember,' she says. 'But I tell you, he is changing; he will continue to change. A nice, caring email from you will touch him and make him even more willing to change.'

I write the email, because it matters to her that I do. I write it because perhaps she has a point. I write:

> Dear Papa, Mama just told me that you have not been feeling well and have been in the hospital often. I wanted to wish you a speedy recovery. If there's anything I can do, please let me know. Please get some rest and get well soon. Sincerely, Uchenna

I read it to her over the phone. She approves, gives me his email address, tells me to go ahead and send it. 'You're a good daughter,' she says. 'A really good daughter, with a really good heart. Sometimes it's the young people who have to teach the old,' she says.

'Yeah, yeah,' I say, but I am smiling now, and I am hopeful that she is right. I imagine a clearer future for us. An image of the sun comes into my head, and I think that maybe this whole thing is like when you've been staring straight into the sunlight for some time, and then you look away and your vision is blurry, your eyes confused, but then you continue to look away for not even a few more seconds and suddenly your eyes focus again.

I reason that maybe not always focusing on Papa's bad

behaviour, not always remembering, not always staring the past in the face, maybe this is all it'll take to mend things. Maybe the problem is mine, has been mine all along. Maybe I just need to let go of the past, looking only indirectly, if at all, at the sun.

'You're a good daughter,' she says again. 'A good daughter.' And then she tells me she has to get back to work.

The next day, after dinner, I open up my email and see that he has responded. He says:

Daughter, the path to a fulfilling and beneficial future is not the utter disrespect of your father and your mother. As a child, it is your duty to accept the discipline of your parents, regardless of whether you agree or disagree. Of course, as an adult, you are free to determine your own path, based purely on your selfish desires. For my part, I also have a right not to condone or support that path. The least you can now do is to reconsider your ways, and then toe a path that will reconcile you with the father who gave you life. For starters, you should stop moving in and out sneakily whenever you want to see your mother. You think I do not know, but I know. Entering my house without my permission is the ultimate sign of the utter disappointment that you are. You must at some point begin to take responsibility for your choices, actions and conduct. You hurt nobody but yourself, and you cannot later turn around to blame anyone else.

Father

His response sets me off. I wonder how he is able to box up all his abuse under the category of discipline. Does his conscience really tell him that discipline is all that it has been? As for sneaking around with Mama, I want to tell him that normal children are not forced to sneak around to see their mothers, because normal fathers would never ban their children from coming to their houses, especially not for the reason that he has banned me. I have not been disrespectful, I want to scream. 'How have I been disrespectful?' I whisper to myself.

I pick up the phone and call Mama. I don't say hello, and I don't wait for her to say hello. First, I read my email again to her. Immediately after, I read his response.

'Oh, no, no, no!' she exclaims.

'This is how he's changed?' I ask.

She's silent for a while. Then she clears her throat. 'I'm sorry,' she says.

I tell her I have to go, and I hang up the phone.

All that was over five years ago, almost six years now, and a part of me wants to scold myself for remembering, wants to ask myself why I haven't forgotten all about it by now.

She doesn't need to give him my number, I mutter to myself. There's no way that I'll let her give him my number. In my head, I am remembering all the emails that followed that first one. They grew angrier and angrier, probably spurred on by the fact that I refused to respond – one-line emails about how I was allowing Satan to guide me, about my being a blockhead, about how I would amount to nothing.

I am wearing a pair of jeans and a loose white dress shirt. I wipe my sweaty palms on the bottom half of the shirt, and the moisture from my hands leaves a wet mark. I call Mama back on my cell phone.

'You can't give him my number,' I say, as soon as she picks up.

'Why not?' Mama asks, sounding a little irritated.

'That would be like an invitation for attack,' I tell her.

'It's not that serious,' Mama says.

'It is,' I say.

She says, 'Not now. I'm very busy here at work, handing out medication, filling out paperwork and other things. Now is not the time.'

I say, 'It was a mistake back then to give him access to my email address. He sent all those angry emails, remember?'

She stays silent.

'You call him yourself and find out when he's ready. Then call me back and tell me, and I'll get the food ready. But whatever you do, please don't give him my number.'

'Don't call trouble where there is no trouble,' she says. Then she tells me she has to go and hangs up the phone.

I know that he usually eats dinner at 6.30 p.m. At 6 p.m. I head into the kitchen and dish out the yam and spinach pottage onto a glass plate. I cover the plate with another glass plate and stick it in the microwave. I program in two and a half minutes, but I don't hit the START button.

On the kitchen counter, I set out the plastic plate onto which I will transfer the food. I set out plastic utensils next to the plastic plate, and I fill a big plastic cup with water. I walk back to my room, a quick step into my bathroom, and then I lounge on my bed, waiting to hear from Mama about when he is ready to eat.

At 6.30, I think I hear the clicking sound of a door being shut, but I don't hear anything else, no footsteps, no sounds of movement. I don't think much of the clicking, but all the same, I decide to walk out of my room and into the kitchen to push START on the microwave, to finish the preparation so that in case he comes to check for his food, it will be all ready for him.

I enter the kitchen and the first thing I see is that the plastic plate, cup and utensils are no longer on the counter. I open the microwave and see that the food is no longer there. Instead there are two empty glass plates in the sink, the plates on which I had dished out the food, the plates on which the food would have been heated up.

Hours later, about nine o'clock, my cell phone rings, and Mama is on the line. 'So you took the food to him?' she asks.

'No,' I say. 'By the time I went to finish up the preparation, he had already come and taken it himself. I'm surprised I didn't even hear the microwave beeping when he finished heating up the food.'

She is quiet on the line.

'I must have been in the bathroom,' I tell her.

She is still quiet.

'Mama?' I say. 'Are you still there?'

'Yes,' she says. 'But you disappoint me. I don't ask you for much, but this is radiation we're talking about. It would not have killed you to let me give him your number. For God's sake, it is radiation we're talking about.'

I say, 'Mama, I couldn't handle the possibility of getting harassing calls or text messages from him on my phone.'

'All you had to do was just let me give him your number, so that you would have known when to prepare the food, when to place it for him on that table by his door. Is it too much for me to ask you to prepare his food for him? It's not like I was asking you to cook it. All I was asking was for you to dish it out.'

'No,' I say. 'It was not too much to ask. And I didn't mind preparing the food. But Mama,' I say, 'why didn't you call him? Why didn't *he* call me from his doorway, like he's done before? He could have stood there and just told me that he was ready for his food.'

'You could have just allowed me to give him your number,' Mama says.

'There you go again,' I say. 'Always putting him first. Always putting his needs before mine.'

'Putting his needs first?' she asks. 'I've never once put his needs before yours.'

I think of Boston and the Florida trip, of him hitting her, and still she went back to serve him a second time. And all the while neither she nor I ate. I think of my bleeding lips, and of her telling me not to say anything to the cops. *Do you want to be responsible for sending a diabetic man to jail?* I think of sneaking in and out of the house, because Mama did not want to anger him by demanding that I be allowed to come back home. I think of writing that email. Of being here now at the house.

She says, 'He could have contaminated the items in the kitchen with his radiation. You think I was concerned for him when I asked you to prepare the meal for him? No,' she says. 'My concern was for you and for me. Not wanting the radiation to seep out to us. And here you are telling me how I put him before us.'

I tell her that if she was so concerned for our safety, she could have done as I had suggested; she could have called him and then gotten back to me with a time when he would be expecting to have the meal.

'You disappoint me,' she tells me. 'Accusing me of catering to him, as if I don't have a head of my own, as if I don't have my own priorities.'

I don't answer. Instead, I sit on my bed, shaking my head slowly from side to side.

A few nights later, he calls my name from his room, like he did the days following the first procedure, the surgery.

Those times, his request was simple: he only asked for a glass of water.

I imagine he is by their bedroom door, standing at the top of the three steps that lead into his room. My room is past the living room, down the hallway, on the opposite side of the house. My door is only a crack open, so I don't see him, but I imagine that he's wearing his blue-and-white-striped pyjama pants and his white singlet. He screams my name, though not really screaming, just shouting it so that I can hear. 'Uchenna!' he says.

I have just come out of the bathroom. I have tossed the towel on my bed, and I am unfolding a pad from its plastic wrapping, about to stick it onto my underwear. It is past 10 p.m.; by now, he should be sleeping.

I look at my door, and it occurs to me that I am completely nude, and that he could, in that very moment, be making his way slowly to my door. So I respond hurriedly, in order to catch him on time. 'I'm not dressed,' I say. 'I can't come out right now.'

His response comes right away, without even a moment of hesitation.

'Don't you dare snap at me,' he shouts. 'Don't you dare!' Then, 'If you know what's best for you, better put on your clothes and get me a glass of water!' He clears his throat loudly and adds, 'Or else.'

For a moment, I want to explain myself to him. I want to tell him that he shouldn't be angry with me, because I did not mean any of it disrespectfully. But before I can get my mouth to open up, I hear his footsteps fading away, and then I hear his door slam shut.

I sit on my bed, holding the pad in my hands, imagining colourful butterflies, mutated butterflies filling up all the empty space in my room. I imagine tumours on many of them, and frightful metamorphoses of each and every tumour that I see, so that in the end, the diseased butterflies can hardly be separated from the healthy ones. I cringe. I feel the blood from my insides dripping out. I imagine that it is staining the yellow sheet under me. But I don't do a thing to thwart the stain.

The next day, I pack my bags and prepare to leave. Mama stands at my doorway and watches me fold my blouses, watches me place them into my suitcase.

'I still need you here,' she says. It comes out dry, monotone. 'I don't see why you're leaving so suddenly.'

I place the blouse that I am holding in the suitcase. I turn around so that I am facing her, looking straight into her eyes. I say, 'You are an emotionally abusive mother whose greatest function in my life has been to perpetuate your husband's abuse. It has always been and always will be about him. About not making him angry, about taking care of him, about giving him food this way and that. He will always be your number one priority. And so, you see, I have no business being here.'

I surprise myself, because it's not as if I've ever thought of any of this before. I surprise Mama, too. 'Hush,' she says. 'Don't say such foolish things!'

But I insist. 'No, Mama,' I say. 'It's really true. I mean every word of it. Catering to an abusive person is one thing, but forcing others to do the same, whatever your reasons, is its own form of abuse.'

She raises one hand to her face, covers her eyes with it. 'You accuse me of being emotionally abusive?' she asks. Her voice is soft, as if she's pleading, as if she's hoping that I'll change my mind and come up with a different verdict about her.

I look at her, just watch her. I don't say a thing.

'Me?' she begins again, her voice breaking. 'You really think that I have been emotionally abusive to you?'

'Yes, Mama,' I say. It is then that her shoulders begin to shake. I know that she is crying, that what I said really is hurting her.

'Me?' she asks one last time. She mumbles, and somewhere in the middle of the blubbering, I think I hear her say something about life being all about sacrifices.

She really gets into the crying now, her shoulders heaving, her breath catching and releasing, catching and releasing. I look at her, she is pitiful, and something in me wants to enjoy this moment. Something in me wants to smile and say, 'Now you feel what I feel.' But then I look at her again. And she looks more pitiful than she has ever looked all the times that Papa hit her or screamed at her. More pitiful than she looked even with her black eye in Boston. It occurs to me that *I* am the one making her feel this way. And I realize that it's not at all something to smile about.

'Anyway, he's back to normal now,' I say. 'You really don't need me any more.'

She shakes her head, tells me that she does. She needs me more than I can imagine, she says. She cries hard, and her voice trembles, but I don't allow the tears or the trembling to sway me. Instead, I stand there, robot-like; and as I watch her sobbing continue, it begins to feel like something is being lifted out of me, something heavy and light at once. She is begging me to stay, but I barely hear the words. Instead, I'm imagining that that thing in me is fluttering away.

He comes out of their bedroom as I am about to take my luggage down the stairs, in the direction of the front door. I pretend that I do not notice him.

When I am midway down the staircase, he says, 'Once you

leave, don't think you can come back. You're not welcome here unless I say you are.'

I walk the rest of the way down the staircase. And I think that one day, God willing, I will have a husband and at least one child of my own. And chances are that my husband and I won't always see eye to eye. So, maybe sometimes I'll find myself yielding to him, because, after all, I'll love him very much. Still, I'll love him not quite as much as I'll love my child.

I grab hold of the door knob and pull open the door. Outside, the sky is blue and white. I can feel a soft breeze, and I can feel the warmth of the sun on my skin.

'Do you hear me?' Papa asks as I step out. 'Don't think you can set foot here again without my permission. You understand?'

I turn back in his direction, and I nod, a slow and wistful nod. And I wonder if he even knows why I'm leaving.

Acknowledgements

I am grateful to my friends, mentors and teachers at Penn State, Rutgers, the Iowa Writers' Workshop, and elsewhere. You are too many to list, but you know yourselves.

Special thanks to Jan Zenisek, Deb West and David, the custodian.

Special thanks also to Rae Winkelstein, Lori Martin, Montreux Rotholtz, Emily Ruskovich, Michael Martone, Robin Hemley, Allan Gurganus and Marilynne Robinson.

Heartfelt thanks to Jin Auh, Ellah Allfrey and Jenna Johnson, for believing so strongly in me.

John Freeman, I'm not sure where I would be without you. My most heartfelt thanks to you.